DEDICATION

To Tom, my inspiration, best friend, and forever love.

She didn't know how he'd found out, but since he had, she had to leave...and fast!

It was obvious from his words that evening that the self-proclaimed beautiful people disgusted him. Whether she'd been a willing participant or truly a victim was immaterial. She had been a part of the set, and for that there was no excuse.

Stifling a sob of what she was sure was relief, she fell against the driver's door. It was unlocked, as always when she was out of the city, and the keys would be in the ignition. She eased open the door, reaching immediately to turn off the interior light, and rested gratefully against the seat.

In just a minute, she would get into the seat, turn the key and flip the levers that would blow heat off the engine. With her injured ankle, getting into the motorhome would be difficult, but she had come too far now to give up. She straightened, bracing one hand on the seat, curling the other around the steering column, below the ignition and the dangling key ring.

But the keys weren't there.

Muttering dire threats to the missing keys, she released the steering column, ducking under the wheel to check the floor beneath the seat. It was awkward but there was no other way to check, especially without a light.

Illumination was provided suddenly, when the passenger door was flung open, and the beam of a powerful flashlight was aimed directly into her face.

"Looking for something, Ms. Acton?"

Her past was behind her...or so she'd thought.

Bethany Acton has come a long way from the day she was an abused child-bride of a dissolute jet setter. Now divorced and single, she writes for a lifestyles magazine, lives out of her motor home, and answers only to her boss—when he can find her. She has overcome her horrendous past and taken control of her own life. But when Jonathan Merritt, a rising star in wildlife photography, enters her world, she learns that *control* is a tenuous thing.

His past was despicable, but it hasn't affected his future...until now.

Jonathan knows he has met the woman with whom he wants to spend his future, but first he must admit his role in her past. Afraid the truth will turn her against him, he tries to gain her trust and affection before confessing. But the longer he hesitates, the harder it becomes to tell her. Can Jonathan gain enough of her love and trust for her to forgive what he did—

or will his past indiscretions destroy his one chance at happiness?

KUDOS for *Teach Me to Forget*

Teach Me to Forget by Mona Karel is a contemporary, hot, and sexy romance about a young woman who was abused by her first husband. Bethany breaks away from her tycoon husband and starts her life over, only to fall in love with a man involved setting her up for that abuse in the first place...I was a little unclear as to when exactly Jonathan realizes that Bethany is the same person he inadvertently helped set up for her teenage wedding, but other than that, I had few complaints about the story. The writing is good, the plot strong, and the characters charming. This is a story about overcoming your past, learning from your mistakes, and forgiving others who also learn from theirs. – *Taylor, reviewer*

Teach Me to Forget by Mona Karel is an interesting novel. While it doesn't have the same paranormal thriller bent that her first novel, *My Killer, My Love* had, it does have the same injured/scarred heroine, aloof/unfeeling hero style that appealed to me so much in that book. In the case of *Teach Me to Forget*, the heroine Bethany is emotionally and psychologically injured rather than physically, but the wounds are deep and just as debilitating as physical ones...The writing in *Teach Me to Forget* is as good as in *My Killer, My Love*, and the plot is equally strong. The subject matter was handled with sensitivity and the sex scenes are hot. – *Regan, reviewer*

TEACH ME TO FORGET

by

MONA KAREL

A BLACK OPAL BOOKS PUBLICATION

GENRE: CONTEMPORARY ROMANCE/
WOMEN'S FICTION

This is a work of fiction. Names, places, characters and incidents are either the product of the author's imagination or are used fictitiously, and any resemblance to any actual persons, living or dead, businesses, organizations, events or locales is entirely coincidental.

PROLOGUE

Summer 2000:

It was a storybook wedding. The elite of the world's beautiful people crowded the groom's yacht, cruising off the south French coast. The groom's austere face was only slightly lined, the gray at his temples adding a distinguished air. His still trim body was clothed by the establishment which had enjoyed the patronage of every male in his family since his great-grandfather. Although he conversed urbanely with his guests, his possessive gaze never left his bride.

Framed in the lens of the ever-clicking camera, the bride had the lithe slenderness seen only in the very young and healthy. Delicate curves hinted at the woman she would one day become. Her short dark hair was gamine cut by the stylist who had created the look. Her make-up had been applied by the hands of the genius whose company had taken three generations of women from beautiful to gorgeous. Her lavish bouquet was of rare miniature white orchids, picked deep in the rain forests of South America and flown in for this ceremony. The lace for her veil had been created by devout hands in a convent which had produced lacework of this gossamer perfection for centuries.

The veil was secured by a pearl crown once belonging to a medieval princess. It framed a delicate, serious face dominated by enormous, hazy green eyes and a lush, slightly trembling mouth, and billowed down to hand made, four inch spike heels. By tradition the full length veil attested to the purity of the bride, leaving no doubt in the mind of anyone attending that day that this was, indeed, a virgin bride. The diaphanous covering enhanced her bridal outfit, personally designed by the hand of the dresser of royalty. Brilliant fire opals had been meticulously applied to the hand sewn, French cut white bikini.

CHAPTER 1

Ten years later, the offices of Western Living Magazine, *San Francisco, California*:

"A cton, are you done in there yet?"

Bethany Acton stared at herself in the fogged-over mirror, and wondered exactly what her boss, Neil Chandler, meant by done? She was done removing the grime collected in the last three days, when showers were not possible.

Her skin, now concealed by the navy blue T-shirt she'd pulled on over a sturdy, dark sports bra, had attained an interesting shade of pink. Nearly the same pink tracked across the whites of her eyes, providing more color than their usual indeterminate green.

She was even done subduing her stubborn mass of hair, too red to be a proper shade of brunette, into a semblance of restraint. She was also done looking at herself in the mirror.

She'd been done with that for a long, long time.

"You can't hide in there forever, Acton."

Who could ignore such a perfect entry cue? Securing an olive green scarf around her still damp hair, she added a matching over-blouse and reached for the bathroom door. At the last minute she dropped a battered fatigue cap on her head. Neil hated her cap.

"Who said anything about hiding? The heater's out in my rig and I had to use your shower." She spoke airily as she moved into the room, trying to project enthusiasm. "I've got to talk to you about a piece I want to do. Celia said you were out with someone. She told you I was here, didn't she?"

"She didn't have to." Neil indicated the regularly spaced smudges, reaching from the office entrance to the bathroom, on the thick, elegantly pale gray carpeting. The luxurious office was a testimony to his transition from renowned wire service reporter to highly successful magazine editor. Along the way he'd gained some weight, lost some hair, and almost learned how to deal with the likes of BL Acton. "I take it you parked in the under-ground."

4

She spared a moment's regret for the carpet, but an apology could be taken as a weakness. At this point she needed to negotiate from a position of power. She had to remain focused.

"Of course. I wouldn't leave my rig in front of the building and risk lowering the property value. Your messages sounded serious, so I decided to come straight in. I would have skipped going to Paul's but..."

"If you thought the messages sounded so serious, why didn't you bother returning one or two of them?" Neil kept his voice calm but the effort was beginning to show.

"I was coming in anyway?" Slanting a glance at him, she wondered if her editor was in a mood to be charmed right now or if she needed to give him more time to rant.

Neil caught the look, probably recognizing it as one his daughters and, more recently, his granddaughters, had tried out on him. Giving way to a gust of laughter, he lifted his hands in surrender but continued in a serious tone.

"Acton, we put a telephone in your motorhome to ensure communication. You're my only writer without a house or apartment. I must be able to reach you."

"You've never worried before about where I was, as long as you had my itinerary."

"Your 'itinerary' tells me where you might be within a span of three to four days. Unless we have answers from some of your contact numbers, we have no idea where you are."

"I still don't understand what the big deal is," she muttered, wandering over to his massive desk.

Her boss gathered his control with an obvious effort. Bethany knew she could send him off on a tangent faster than any revolutionary head of state.

"Do you remember the piece you did for Steve Wilkins while his wife was in the hospital?"

"The review of J. Phillip Merritt's latest book?" She tried to keep her voice casual. "I thought it was a rather good piece of writing. As I remember you agreed, at least on the final version."

"We've had some negative feedback."

She frowned, turning to face him completely.

"You've only sent out advance copies, haven't you? What was the objection, that I'd seen the great man's book, or that I enjoyed it?"

Neil didn't answer her directly. Turning his head slightly, he nodded to someone behind her.

"The fact, Ms. Acton, that the review was written at all."

The voice, clear and commanding with just a hint of an accent, came from a grouping of plush leather chairs near the window. Bethany cursed her lack of attention. No wonder she hadn't been able to charm Neil. On the outer fringes of her conscious, she'd sensed trouble.

Trouble came very elegantly packaged these days. The slightly baggy linen slacks were the *dernier cri* among those people to whom these things mattered more than life or sanity. For just a moment, as the tall, lean frame unfolded, backlit by the sunny San Francisco afternoon, she experienced an unpleasant shock of near recognition. Then he attained his full height and the impression was gone.

He strolled forward—the look, one she knew all too well. His hair, dark and thick with an artistic droop over his high brow, wasn't quite as meticulous as might be expected. But she'd been isolated too long to be up on all the nuances—slightly rumpled could be all the rage this year. Certainly his pale blue eyes were ideal to convey his emotions, or lack thereof. She quelled an irrational impulse to step back. She'd stopped backing off about the same time she'd stopped studying herself in mirrors.

If she had retained the primitive escape impulses, she'd have indulged herself now. The stranger towered over her five-and-a-half-foot height. While his unreadable gaze took in her appearance he leisurely buttoned a European tailored jacket, automatically smoothing the sleeves. He had elegant hands, lean and strong-looking, with deft fingers. She didn't want those hands anywhere near her body. Neil stepped between them, a welcome buffer in an atmosphere suddenly overloaded with tension.

"Lose the hat, Acton," Neil muttered, pushing a cup of coffee into her stiff right hand. As if he knew she wouldn't want to offer her hand in greeting.

With her free hand, she plucked the well-worn hat from her head, flicking it onto a chair. The scarf was revealed, covering her hair completely and doing nothing for her appearance. Neil's groan came between clenched teeth.

"J. Phillip Merritt, BL Acton."

Bethany felt her breath catch sharply in her throat. Her interest had been strictly in the renowned nature photographer's work. Had she thought about the man himself, her image of him might have been along the lines of someone of sufficient size to equal the majesty of the images he preserved. She might have envisioned a fussy older sort, excruciatingly precise about detail and prone to wearing sweaters with shiny suede patches on the elbow.

Never would she have pictured a man fashionably dressed, with the kind of leanly muscled body made to wear the most expensive clothing—or no clothing at all. Shocked by this unaccustomed response to a man, she chose to attack rather than allow herself to retreat.

"Mr. Merritt, this is indeed an honor. I was not aware you moved among mortals."

"Acton," warned Neil.

"Were you aware that I prefer not to have my work reviewed in advance of publication?" Merritt asked, as though only mildly interested.

Bethany realized avoiding a handshake wouldn't be a problem. He'd jammed his hands into the pockets of his slacks, no doubt to keep from wrapping them around her neck. She had that effect on a lot of people. From the corner of her eye she thought she caught a questioning expression on Neil's face, but when she turned her head to look more closely, he was back to his enigmatic reporter look.

"In particular," Merritt continued, still in that indifferent tone, "I do not encourage reviews done by unknown, imitation bohemians of questionable talent."

"Would this mean you prefer reviews done by genuine, notorious bohemians?" She felt a brief moment of chagrin when Merritt's mouth tightened, making his expression seem even more severe. This was the man who'd photographed dawn through a frozen spider web? He seemed to have the sensitivity of a glacier.

"Acton, have you eaten lately?" Neil broke in gamely, probably trying to excuse her testy mood. A frown was gathering on his brow, as though he were confused by something.

"How could I? Your phone's been hounding me since last night." Hearing the acid in her voice she turned away and drew a deep breath. When possible, a wise negotiator avoided confrontation on more than one front. "I think I had lunch yesterday." She turned back before her boss could utter his standard protest. "But I'm taking my vitamins."

"We were waiting lunch until you got here."

Bethany eyed Merritt's elegant clothing, and his expression. How had Jane Austen described Darcy? Repulsive? Repugnant? That was the problem with a classical education; she remembered just enough to confuse herself. Whatever, J. Phillip Merritt looked every bit the part of a supercilious aristocrat, as though he'd just stepped out of an historical novel. A deep rooted imp took over her vocal cords.

"I get the impression, Neil, that Mr. Merritt would not feel comfortable being seen in public with the likes of me." She'd expected at best a smirk in reaction. What she got looked almost like a brief, guilty flush.

"Marsha found an outfit she thought you might like," Neil said, still determinedly cheerful. "If you want to change we could try the new seafood place."

"The dark green silk in the closet? It's lovely. I thought I recognized your wife's taste." She hadn't seen anything that stunning in many years. Then again, she no longer had use for that kind of camouflage. "I could stay like I am and order in a pizza."

"How about a light lunch at the French place down the street?"

"How about I grab a 'cheeseboogie' or something and meet you back here?" She was almost able to smile. Neil was beginning to melt a little. If she could just get safely through the confrontation with Merritt—from the look on the photographer's lean face, she wasn't sure how easy that would be.

Neil looked from one antagonist to the other, and sighed. Between her fondness for mischief and the aloof photographer's lack of appreciation for her lively tongue, Neil had to know it might not be a pleasant meal. The least he could do was pick a restaurant where they'd all be comfortable.

"There's a small place a few blocks away, Mr. Merritt," Neil said, apparently catching on. "Good selection, fresh food and patio tables. The dress code is relaxed but you might want to bring along your hat in case we're in the sun."

❧❧❧

The food was superb, the service unobtrusive. Between courses, Jonathan Phillip Merritt sipped at freshly brewed coffee, watching the Acton woman while she pretended to concentrate on an excellent thick soup.

She'd chosen a table in the corner, seating herself against a brick wall softened by dark vines. Since her irreverent behavior in the office she'd refused to acknowledge his existence, determinedly keeping Chandler between them on the brisk walk to the restaurant. Once there, she chose to sit out of his direct line of sight.

Jonathan wondered if BL Acton thought wearing layers of ill-fitting clothing was sufficient armor against a curious male population. Her fluid movement hinted at a fascinating body. She dressed in Goodwill surplus but carried herself like a graduate from an outstanding private school.

He remembered a flash of thick auburn hair below the fatigue cap when she first sailed into the office, covered in mud and insouciance while she navigated through the greetings of her co-workers. Her zest for life, her intense vitality, had been obvious even from across the room.

From that distance and under a coating of various shades of dust and grime, her features seemed unremarkable. Cleaned up, her hair concealed, her face was displayed severely. A light golden tan, fine bones, a dainty nose and soft mouth couldn't be disguised no matter how obsessively unfeminine she tried to look. Dark, thick brows and lashes guarded large eyes that made him think of his favorite secluded forest glade. She hadn't quite hidden the flash of apprehension in her mossy green eyes when she noticed him for the first time. When she learned his identity, her guilt was obvious, and charming.

Her persona was excellent, the hard-driven, carefree, field reporter, sailing through life with a joke and a byline. It lacked only a can of beer in her fist to complete the picture. Still, no calloused, shallow reporter could have produced a review that cut effortlessly to the very soul of his work.

She was bantering again with Neil, the tension momentarily leaving her soft, full mouth when she heard a story about the newest member of the Chandler clan. As though suddenly coming to a decision Neil reached out, not quite touching her arm.

"Why don't you spend some time at our place while you're in town? You can have that corner room that opens onto the patio."

This brought a wistful expression to her delicate features. For a moment she seemed tempted, one side of her soft lower lip slipping in between her teeth while she considered the offer. Jonathan felt an almost uncontrollable urge to rescue the abused lip, and hold it for ransom between his own teeth. The thought made him stir restlessly. This made no sense. Smart-mouthed females in masculine dress, who made a career out of being tougher and quicker than anyone else, held no appeal for him. Much to his relief, she released her lip.

"Who's going to be there this week, Neil?" she asked, her voice silky, eyebrows slightly raised.

"Marsha, the girls. You know, the usual." Neil murmured, suddenly very nonchalant.

"Mmm, I do know. What night is she planning the party?"

For a moment, Neil seemed irritated then he laughed abruptly. "That depends on what night you're planning to be there. You know Marsha, she never gives up."

"Well, give her my love and thanks for her concern, but I think I'll bow out. I'm not up to facing the madding crowd right now. Besides, Casey'll be coming by tonight or tomorrow."

"For what?" Neil seemed to be confused, but his voice was a shade too smug.

"That piece I was trying to tell you about earlier." She looked at him over the rim of her coffee cup, tilting her head in question. "Why else would I want to see him?"

Her air of innocence was almost perfect, but Jonathan saw the shy imp peering out from behind the shadows in her eyes. Acton was baiting her boss and seemed to enjoy every second of it. Until he noticed the death grip she had on her coffee cup.

"You wouldn't be planning to ask him about the photos he took for this next issue, by any chance?" Neil leaned forward in his chair, arms on the table edge. He was beginning to establish control over the situation.

"Oh," she breathed, all flutter-headed innocence. "You've seen those?"

"I approved them. Not a bad piece, Acton. You really got into that man's character."

Acton waved aside the praise that, from her heightened color, warmed her intensely. "What about the shot by the fireplace?" she asked, as though it were of no great interest.

"Good composition, marvelous color. I particularly liked the way the firelight filters through the dog's ears. You could have done a bit more with your appearance but it does a lot for your image as a hard driven independent."

"We had a deal, remember?" The breathy voice was gone, replaced by a clarity of tone that would do justice to a lawyer. "I would find the people who were hiding out from the world and display them in your magazine. In exchange my privacy would be ensured. 'The Lone Interviewer,' you called me. You liked the idea of me being a mystery person, remember? I was willing to overlook the fact

17

that my back was 'inadvertently' not cropped out of one shot—"

"Not quite your whole back, as I remember," Neil broke in smoothly, refilling his coffee cup from the carafe. "Do you by any chance remember what preceded that issue?" The tolerant humor had left Neil's voice, to be replaced by the stern tones of an irate headmaster.

"That was when you found out I was turning off my car phone," she said quietly, her shoulders slumping.

What had been a lightly accented, almost musical, voice suddenly lost all inflection. Only then did Jonathan realize how pleasant she had sounded. The cultured tones and precise pronunciation were as much at odds with the impression she attempted to convey as were the fine boned wrists extending from the cuffs of her heavy cotton over-shirt.

There was more than frustrated ego here. BL Acton was genuinely disturbed that the layout draft of her most recent article was accompanied by a photograph of her. The sudden haunted look in her eyes reminded Jonathan more than ever of a wood sprite thrust into the middle of civilization. Then her chin raised, her back straightened, and the sprite was sent back to hide in the enchanted forest.

Neil let the silence stretch until it became uncomfortable for all of them before he spoke again. "Relax, Acton. There are alternates for that shot. However," he continued sternly, "I can and will use that photo in the future if you do not keep in touch."

He didn't speak again until the young woman looked up and nodded tightly. "Tell me," he asked, seeming genuinely interested. "Why would you want to talk to Casey? I choose the photos."

"That's true, but he takes them." She allowed herself to relax and some of the beauty returned to her voice, along with the playful gleam in her eyes. "Casey knows I believe in getting even," she said smugly, checking the carafe then signaling for fresh coffee. It was obvious she had fulfilled her purpose for the lunch meeting, and she was ready to eat quickly and get away.

She was ignoring him. Jonathan could not believe it at first, but this audacious fashion disaster was pretending he did not exist. He'd been willing to wait, to be patient as Chandler suggested, until she could get any pressing business out of the way and begin to relax. Obviously, patience was not going to get the job done.

He directed his attention to Chandler while Acton was occupied with the waitress. A lifted eyebrow, a shrugged shoulder, a nod of the head, and Chandler was setting down his napkin and rising. "Excuse me a minute. No, don't get up, Acton. I see someone over there I've been trying to get in touch with for days. Marsha needs a commitment from him for one of her charities. You don't mind taking over for me, do you?"

❧❧❧

Neil left without waiting for an answer, walking away before Bethany could even get her lips moving. It wasn't really a problem. Acting like a gracious hostess was one thing for which she had actually been trained. She opened her mouth, certain that an innocuous statement would fall out automatically. It never had a chance.

"It is interesting to note, Ms. Acton, that you are so protective about your own privacy and so careless about someone else's." Merritt's cold haughty voice was in keeping with her initial image of him.

"The book was sent to us," she said, tightly. So much for gracious.

"In error, and the publisher wrote you to that effect."

"Not soon enough, I'm afraid." She strove for absolute perfection in word and phrase. "Our regular reviewer was out that month, and I was filling in. By the time that letter arrived I was out of pocket, I believe on a working dude ranch, or was it the lost gold mine? Whichever, the letter caught up to me long after the piece was done and the magazine was in print."

Actually, the letter, addressed simply to the book reviewer, had ended up in her pocket, unopened. The chance to write about her favorite photographer's work had been too good to pass up. An apology, if required, had seemed a modest price to pay. Now she wondered. J. Phillip Merritt unnerved her. It had been years since she'd been close to a man like this, and she'd forgotten most of her hard-learned defenses.

"You do realize, Ms. Acton, I could have gone directly to the owners of the magazine. I doubt they would be quite so cavalier about this matter. Trouble for your editor would be an extreme price to pay for a practical joke, wouldn't you say?"

At the threat to her friend she stiffened, chin raising, banishing any pretense of humor from her deliberately haughty expression. Power grew in her, overcoming the fear, drawing strength from the kind of education available only to the elite few. At times she had despised that education, but for this moment she welcomed the training.

"Freedom of the press, Mr. Merritt," she began quietly, not allowing her voice to change from the perfectly modulated tones. "At worst, I would have to print a retraction. Let me see, how would I word this?" She narrowed her eyes, drawing her brows together, giving every impression of serious thought. From deep inside came a need to strike out at this man, to push him away before he could get any closer.

"In spite of my former review, I have not seen J. Phillip Merritt's latest offering. I do not feel his talent is of any significance.

Surely any hack with a box camera can do a better job of portraying the fragile beauty of the environment." She drew in a breath, fighting the quaver her voice acquired when she let herself become upset. "Nor do I sense any emotion when I happen to encounter his work, except perhaps the feeling that he is a pompous ass."

She rose from her chair, turning away from the table, nearly stepping into her editor. "Neil, I have a few things to take care of, so I'll be off now. I'll have them wrap my sandwich to go. If you need me, you know where I'll be parked." Her dignity still protected her like a cloak. "If Mr. Merritt has need of any further communication, you might inform him I specialize in mature, interesting people. Perhaps an interview could be arranged—in ten or twenty years."

She avoided Neil's outstretched hand and dropped crumpled dollar bills on the table before turning away. She was aware of the flare of interest in Merritt's glittering blue eyes but chose to ignore it. After today, she would continue to admire Merritt's body of work but she had no interest in seeing any more of his body.

Jonathan enjoyed the rear view picture of her winding through closely packed tables, her spine erect, her head carried just so. A diamond in the rough. No, not quite. A diamond of the first quality, roughly faceted by a careless hand. The chilling thought came from somewhere deep within him. No, he argued with himself. The tension-tightened mouth and shadows in her eyes had been a trick of the light, nothing more.

He felt eyes boring into him, and turned to face the humor on Neil Chandler's face.

"She needs manners," Jonathan murmured, knowing the older man wasn't fooled.

"Her manners are impeccable. She just chooses when to use them."

Jonathan toyed with the handle of his coffee cup, contemplating the money that had been flung on the table. Even in that small way, she proclaimed her self-reliance. "What do you know about her?"

"I know she is a very private person," Chandler began, obviously choosing his words carefully. "I know she writes better than anyone else on my staff, and I'm very lucky she wants to stay with us. She has a knack for finding and interviewing people I didn't know existed. One day she'll realize there's more to the world than California and this magazine, and we'll lose her.

"My family adores her," he continued, now smiling at some private thought. "My wife would adopt her in an instant if she could. Beyond that I can't tell you. I hired Acton with the agreement that her privacy would not be violated." There was no misunderstanding the finality in his words.

Jonathan sipped his coffee, thinking about forest glades, wounded spirits, wasted lives, and experiences that did not always bear closer inspection. He sensed the blood racing through his veins, gathering energy in anticipation of something momentous.

"Chandler, you know I have never encouraged any press about myself. How would you feel about *Western Living* running an exclusive interview on my life and future plans, to be published in conjunction with my upcoming showing?"

Interest flared in the man across from him, displayed by a covetous gleam in his eyes and a quick stiffening of his spine. It was masked, but not well.

"Who would conduct this interview?"

"I would expect the best, of course."

Now Chandler took time to think. Years of experience with people from all walks of life had honed the editor's instincts. He would have to balance the merits of running this exclusive against the possible negative reaction of a person he valued.

"Do you know what you're getting into?"

Jonathan sat back in his chair, that strange excitement still rushing through his veins. "Yes, I think I do."

"You'll have to pin her down before you can examine her, and no one has ever done that," Chandler advised. "She's unique and very special, and if she were ever intentionally hurt, a lot of people would be very angry."

Jonathan smiled again. For the first time in years, he looked forward to something. "I would never hurt your writer. I'm going to give her a chance to make us both famous," he said and wondered when he had lost his ever-loving mind.

CHAPTER 2

I don't know which one of you looks worse, but I would hazard a guess you and Casey buried the hatchet last night, and not in each other." The receptionist's voice matched the amusement in her eyes.

Bethany shrugged, stifling a yawn. She knew the large pizza and imported beer shared with Casey had taken their toll. After the photographer left she'd tried unsuccessfully to catch up on her sleep. She blamed pizza gremlins and accepted that as a fair payment for an evening spent with someone who appreciated her company. Certainly her restlessness had nothing to do with the exceptional talent and piercing blue eyes that had looked her over briefly and found her lacking.

"Neil in yet?"

"Of course, and asking—"

"Acton, about time you showed up. Keeping banker's hours these days?" The last time

Neil sounded so cheerful, he'd been sending her to a male bikini contest in Venice Beach.

"If bankers kept my hours we wouldn't be having corporation bail outs."

With a sense of *déjà vu*, she entered the office past Neil and met the intense blue eyes of J. Phillip Merritt. He briefly examined her comfortable jeans and loose over-shirt and turned back to his contemplation of the fog just beginning to break up over the city below.

Coffee was passed around, served in bone china cups rather than mugs. Croissants and rolls were set out on a glass tray. Neil was trying for an impression of gentility. Bethany accepted the coffee, ignored the tray, and seated herself as far away from Merritt as she possibly could while remaining in the same room. Neil took a comfortable chair between the two of them, indicating this meeting would be more socializing than business.

The best thing she could do was go along with whatever her editor had planned. Sometimes, Neil liked to pretend she was a socially normal, attention seeking magazine reporter. Sometimes, she let him.

"So glad you could join us this morning, Acton. Did Casey come by, as you expected?"

Neil was using his "soothe the fanatics so they won't notice the article that trashed them" voice. Very smooth, very much in charge. He'd never used the voice on her before, but she'd seen hardened free lancers blanch when they heard it. Wasn't it lucky she'd once been manipulated by someone who made Neil look like an amateur?

"Yes he did, Mr. Chandler. We resolved the matter in question quite adequately." She had finally learned, much to her own satisfaction, that two could play at this game. "He assures me there will not be a repeat of his error."

Usually, when she took on the airs of a grand lady, she got a laugh out of her editor. He seemed to find it highly amusing that she could pretend to be a society matron, and she never bothered to correct him. Neil was not smiling now. Whatever his plans, he wasn't sure if he liked them. It was time to go back to her usual role of brat reporter, or the meeting would go on forever.

"Is there is a purpose behind this meeting, Mr. Chandler? I do have a few more things to do while I'm in the city."

Shaking his head at her, Neil took a delaying sip of coffee before answering. "Yes, there is. Mr. Merritt has agreed to an in-depth interview. We'll shift some things around and run it as the feature for the next issue."

She swung her attention over to the quiet man, so casually elegant in charcoal gray slacks and a fine woven blue linen shirt. He raised an eyebrow, but confined his attention to his coffee. A small smile, not especially pleasant, played around his lips.

"That's quite a departure for Mr. Merritt." Her voice was studiously casual. "Who will be doing the interview?"

"You will, of course. You'll start immediately."

Bethany drew on deep reserves of strength, forcing air into static lungs and concentrating on the rush of oxygen through her system. Most writers would ransom their first born for the opportunity to write about a person of Merritt's growing reputation. All she could think about was being trapped in a situation over which she had no control. Merritt was too much like the kind of person she now avoided.

This was not a hopeless predicament, she reminded herself. No one had control of her life but herself. Not any longer.

"It sounds fascinating, but I leave in four days for Santa Barbara to meet with a rare book dealer. The next stop is in San Diego County, for a tourmaline mine. Then of course there's the shelter story. The earliest I could find time would be in a month or so."

"This needs to be published in conjunction with Merritt's next one-man show," interjected Neil. "You can do the shelter piece immediately after this one. I've spoken with the book dealer and the mine owner; they're willing to wait."

"Well, I'm not!" She knew her anxiety was beginning to show in her tightening voice but couldn't control it. "I can't leave until my heater's fixed, anyway."

"You won't need to stay in your vehicle. There is adequate room at my house." Merritt said, quietly reminding them of his presence.

Bethany surged to her feet, setting her coffee down with a snap that rattled the fine china cup against the saucer.

"I can't stay in your house."

"Ms. Acton, you have no need to fear for your virtue." Merritt's voice was bland enough to be insulting. Most of his attention was on the croissant he'd chosen, and he seemed barely concerned with what was going on.

She felt the heat rising in her face and closed her eyes for a moment to regain her failing grip on her composure. Anger hadn't worked, nor had logic. A deep breath fortified her, so she attempted her final effort.

"I fully realize the opportunity to interview a person of your caliber is indeed an honor, Mr. Merritt," she began smoothly. "However, you must understand that I do not make plans in this arbitrary fashion. I cannot, for instance, ensure that my illustrator will be available on such short notice."

"What need could you possibly have for a photographer?" The man was beginning to sound insufferably pompous.

"Plans have been made for you, Acton," Neil said, his tone final. "There's no purpose in further discussion."

Bethany remembered Merritt's veiled threat. The magazine owners had always been satisfied with Neil, and would never reprimand him on someone else's word. She hoped. Neil and his family were very special to her.

"Very well. Give me directions. I'll start tomorrow."

"There will be no need for directions. My car is being painted. I've wasted two days already waiting for you to decide to check in. The least you can do is give me a lift back."

"I should point out to you that my vehicle is not suitable for running errands, Mr. Merritt."

"That would be no problem. I have another vehicle at my house, which I use locally."

"Well, we can't leave immediately. I have things I need to do before I leave town." Now she was beginning to sound insufferably sullen.

"Do them on the way out." Neil's tolerance was obviously beginning to diminish. "Marsha washed the clothes she kept last time you stayed with us. I believe she also threw in something extra." For just a moment, it seemed as though Neil was smiling smugly. If that were so, it would have been in appreciation of the coup this interview would be for his magazine. He would certainly not be pressuring her as a punishment for refusing to answer her car phone. She decided to give in to the inevitable, but she was damned if she'd be gracious about it.

"Very well. If you want a lift that badly, let's go."

୧୬୧୬

Patience and control. Bethany reminded herself of the lessons learned so long ago. She could handle any situation, as long as she didn't let them get to her. She watched Merritt's face from the corner of her eye as they approached the battered vehicle that had been her home for the last five years. If he had any doubts, he kept them to himself.

He seemed to keep a lot to himself, behind his facade of casual sophistication. It was just as well. If he made a habit of smiling in any fashion but arrogantly, he would have been devastating. Scolding herself for the observation, she dropped the bags from Marsha outside the motorhome door and dug in her pocket for the keys.

"Still want to hitch a ride with me, Mr. Merritt? This is hardly the type of transportation to which you are accustomed."

He stepped back to look over her small motorhome. The paint was faded and there were scrapes where she had gone through rather than around an obstacle. But the tires were excellent, the windows were spotless, and she knew the engine was in exceptional condition. Her question was a subtle insult.

"You're angry about this, aren't you?"

"What was your first clue?" Oops. So much for her damned control.

൞

Hearing the petulant bitterness and juvenile phrasing, Jonathan laughed softly to himself. The self-contained reporter was incensed and not afraid to express herself. She was also aware of how she sounded and had the grace to flush at her own words.

"I dislike being railroaded, Mr. Merritt. If I'd known I had a long drive ahead of me today, I would have arranged to get some serious rest."

His amusement fled as he remembered the tough-bodied young photographer he'd met that morning. She obviously managed to relax the night before—with her buddy Casey.

"Don't worry about me, Ms. Acton. Since you use this as your regular transportation, I doubt I need fear for my safety."

His mood shifted abruptly to icy. She shrugged, turning the key in the lock, as though implying male mood swings were nothing new to her.

"Don't say I didn't warn you. By the way, I hope you like dogs. Yo, Baron, we've got company."

Already aware of some of the discrepancies in the character of this complex, baffling woman, Jonathan stood his ground but prepared to defend himself against a potential attack animal. The door swung wide, revealing a young Irish setter with an intensely deep mahogany-red coat and a madly wagging tail.

"Nothing to worry about," she said, trying not to sound too smug. "Baron is a total flop as a guard dog."

Lifting his bag into the motorhome, Jonathan contemplated the enthusiastic animal. Someone as overburdened with fears and insecurities as Acton seemed to be should have chosen something other than a flop eared, loose-tongued clown.

"Is Baron an adequate companion for you? I would have thought you would own a more suitable guard dog, perhaps a Doberman?"

That deep forest gaze turned on him, shadowed with private memories. Then she looked down at the dog rubbing around her legs. "I will never have one of those around me again," she said tensely, a shudder running visibly up her body. "Baron's fun and silly and devoted to my amusement. I couldn't ask for a better companion."

She lifted her own bags and stepped up into the motorhome, followed closely by her dog. Casually dumping the bags under a table, she moved forward along the narrow aisle, securing cabinets and arranging windows. A few potted plants, showing just enough leaf to identify them as alive, were moved to the sink and the counters were efficiently cleared of anything that could become airborne once they were underway. Settling into the driver's seat and reaching for the seat belt, she looked back over her shoulder briefly.

"Stow your things wherever, Mr. Merritt. Take a seat and strap in. You wanted a ride, you'll get a ride."

ɞɞɞɞ

Jonathan soon discovered that when driving, BL Acton concentrated on her job. She spoke little and drove well, keeping her attention on the road and on a radio news station that offered constant traffic reports. An accident on one of the bridges, delays at every stop, and road work on every main thoroughfare had no effect on her. In many ways, she seemed to be a superior sort of chauffeur.

But no chauffeur he ever met had moved like deep water flowing down a mountain—or had a look that made him itch for his camera and an uninterrupted background. She was not pretty in any popular sense. Her mouth was too tightly held, her expression too remote to overcome the less than classic features she made no effort to enhance. It was her eyes that fascinated him. The few times she would allow herself to look directly at him, they were immeasurable pools of private memories.

He hadn't wanted to photograph a human for over ten years. Now he wanted to fill his camera with images of her and keep them all to himself. The atypical urge baffled him. From the chilling waves of resentment she radiated, he doubted she would sit still long enough for him to use up a single roll of film.

She glanced briefly at him now, the depths of her eyes partially obscured behind dark glasses which could not filter out the indignation in her look. They were in the middle of a traffic snarl, waiting for the construction crew to ponderously maneuver an earth mover across the road. It would be two or three minutes before the flag waver would allow them to advance another ten feet.

"So tell me, Mr. Merritt. When did you decide your car needed painting?"

She seemed more interested in the horse trailer inching along beside them than in his answer. Jonathan didn't allow himself to be fooled. "Yesterday afternoon when you stormed out of the restaurant." He offered the explanation without apology.

"So that's what this is all about?" she asked, incredulous. "Male ego? You couldn't stand the idea that I wasn't fawning all over your exalted self? Did you ever stop to think I might not be interested?"

"Didn't anyone ever teach you the best way to get a man's attention is to ignore him? You certainly do it well enough."

"No, I never did learn that particular lesson, Mr. Merritt. What I learned about were the games men play because they never grew up and they're afraid to grow old. I learned in particular to avoid those games, and the boys who play them. Get out."

She was serious. Her voice was forceful, almost hard. But when she turned to him, the agony on her face and in the depths of her eyes made his stomach clench. Anguish flared from deep within her before she could turn away, staring blindly out the front window.

What had his curiosity and careless arrogance forced her to face? Whatever it was, she was facing it reluctantly, but with great courage. Jonathan realized he had critically miscalculated her, and he cursed the environment that had made him so cynical.

"If I told you I regretted behaving like a pompous ass, would you believe me?"

He knew it was difficult to maintain a high level of anger against someone who so calmly offered a negative opinion of himself. It was particularly difficult when she was trying to avoid being tightly sandwiched between a tractor trailer and a Ferrari. By the time the motorhome was past the roadwork and once more moving forward, she had managed to regain control of herself.

"Why me?" It was a blunt question, asked in a no-nonsense tone of voice.

"You fascinate me?"

"Give it up, Mr. Merritt. You don't need to stroke my ego. I don't have one."

"Everyone has an ego, Ms. Acton." As he spoke, he wondered how accurate his words were. BL Acton seemed to have little awareness of her own value and even less self-confidence. He shifted in his seat, adjusting the shoulder belt. "My career is at a point where I can no longer deny the need for publicity. *Western Living* is a good magazine and you write well. The publishing schedule will work out conveniently with my next gallery showing. The rest—that was just hot air, a male reaction to your attitude. Ignore it."

She glanced in his direction while the road was temporarily clear. "Do you actually know the owners of *Western Living*?"

"No." He concentrated on the scenery. "I never said I did." He could feel the explosion building in her, then she let out her breath in a huff.

"No," she admitted, shaking her head. "You never said you did." Her next glance was almost admiring, as though in recognition of the accomplishment of a fellow manipulator.

As the day progressed it became apparent the drive was wearing on her. She wouldn't complain, and he was learning not to challenge her. They eventually pulled into the nearly empty parking lot of a neatly laid out veterinary clinic, with a small house hidden to one side behind a hedge of roses.

"Last stop, Mr. Merritt. We'll drop off some things here, pick up Baron's groceries, and be on our way to your cabin in the woods."

Before he could respond she was out of her seat and on her way to the rear door, reaching for a case of wine along the way. She had the door opened and was stepping out, balancing the case on one hip, when she turned back.

"In the interest of saving time, would you mind walking Baron? His leash is on the rack there. If you use that grassy spot to the left of the clinic, the staff will clean it up tomorrow."

Jonathan would not allow himself to be put off quite so easily. Shouldering the door closed behind them, he lifted the heavy case of wine out of her arms and waited for her to object. For a moment she apparently considered it then shrugged.

"A few more minutes won't hurt him, I guess," she said almost to herself and turned to lead the way.

Allowing himself a brief moment of pleasure watching what appeared to be an enticingly full derriere moving away, Jonathan followed. Before they reached the clinic door it flew open, allowing the escape of two enthusiastic young Dobermans towing a slender blond.

At another time he might have asked himself why someone so apparently frail would walk two large energetic dogs together and why she would wear a figure revealing designer jumpsuit to do it. For now he rushed forward, wine and all, ready to support Acton when she backed away from the plunging black dogs.

She wasn't backing away. If anything her glide forward and soft greeting were indications of a genuine welcome. The dogs certainly took it that way, dragging their glamorous handler over so they could frisk around Acton's heavy hiking shoes.

"Hello there, kids. Looks like you've grown up a bit." She laughed softly, crouching down to give the dogs access to her face.

"I thought you were afraid of Dobermans," Merritt said. Even to his own ears, his voice sounded lame, confused.

She looked up from being buffeted on both sides by lean heads with enough teeth to dissect her and never miss a lick. Her full lips thinned, the slight smile slipping away as she allowed memory, however briefly, to rule her thoughts.

"Not these goofs. I was there when they were born. In fact, I rubbed at least one of them." As he stared at her in confusion, she attempted what she obviously hoped looked like a small smile. "Caesarean. When the puppies are taken surgically, the mom has no chance to clean them and stimulate their little lungs. Human assistants have to fill in."

⟣⟡⟢

What she did not explain, what she tried not to remember, was her initial fear of the mother, even exhausted by protracted labor. All her mind had been able to see were dogs with dead eyes, their souls bred and trained out of them, whose job it had been to oversee Stefan Dubec's possessions. But the desperation of the moment, the helplessness of the choking black mites had overcome that fear for her and had helped her lay at least one ghost to rest.

She turned her attention to the dogs' chic handler, who didn't seem disposed to linger, though she checked over Merritt with intense feminine curiosity. From the top of her coifed head to dainty feet in inappropriately delicate sandals, the woman looked like she had just stepped out of a salon chair. For the first time in years, Bethany felt as though she were under dressed. She credited this to her exhaustion. Before anything could be said, the clinic door opened abruptly.

Gorgeous would be too meager a word to describe the man who emerged. Thick, sun-kissed golden hair framed a face of timeless Nordic beauty. Brilliant green eyes perused the grouping in the parking lot and some emotion, that might have been relief, came over his classic features. Shoving the papers he held into the pocket of his white lab coat, he rushed forward.

"Darling, you got here!"

❦❦❦

Jonathan could only gape, arms still filled with the damned case of wine, while the man bore down on Acton with every indication of being her lover. It would seem she reciprocated the emotions. At least she wasn't running, screaming, toward the hills. If her response seemed a bit tepid, perhaps she wasn't as passionate a woman as he'd thought. He wondered, too, at the sense of loss that came over him as the doctor took her in a close embrace, turning his back to the rest of the people, shielding his love from the world.

Then Jonathan realized the trendy blond only had a back view. From his own angle, the ardent clasp was sketchy at best, and the doctor's lips were aiming for an ear rather than the tightly compressed mouth. Nor was there an answering embrace. Her slender hands were clenched as though in protest against a broad chest.

❧❧

Bethany willed herself to hold very still, not to react violently to Paul's embrace. There had to be a reason for this. Then his face moved closer, and his chiseled lips nuzzled near her ear. "Help me," he breathed, as desperately as he could and not be overheard.

She understood immediately. Paul was being chased again and his normal polite stalling tactics were obviously not doing any good. If only he didn't enjoy women so much, it would be easier for him to handle them. She slid her hands up to cup his muscular shoulders. Tilting her head back to get a closer look at her friend's face, she fell into her part convincingly, though not with much enthusiasm.

"I'm sorry dear, it took longer than I expected. Have you been waiting long?"

"It wasn't too bad, sweetheart. I had some things to finish up in the clinic. Oh, that reminds me." He pulled some crumpled papers out of his pocket, turning to face the woman he had nearly knocked over a moment before. His free hand remained behind Bethany's back, seeming to be holding her close but actually just barely touching her waist. "Mrs. Lindsay, you forgot Apollo and Thor's shot records. I'm glad I noticed, or you would have had to come back over later."

It was obvious from the way the delicate blond snatched the papers out of his hand that an evening visit had been her plan all along. Bethany stayed close to Paul until the Mercedes wagon was nothing but dust.

"What have you been doing now, you bad person?" she asked, moving away until there was a definite space between herself and her friend.

"Her divorce is almost final. She decided that was the only reason we hadn't achieved a greater closeness." He shuddered then brought himself back to present company. "What are you doing back so soon?" he asked, studying the tall aloof man who stood to one side.

"J. Phillip Merritt, Dr. Paul Emerson. Mr. Merritt needed a ride home."

Paul gave her the kind of look that let her know he wasn't fooled by her flip answer. He reached out a large hand to the stranger then noticed the wine.

"Damn, I'm sorry. Let me take that." The wine changed hands, and they followed him toward the open clinic door. "You'll stay for dinner, won't you?"

She knew without looking Merritt was glowering again. He did it so well. She had warned him about her errands.

"Mr. Merritt needs to get to his house without further delay." A break would have been nice, but Paul's natural curiosity and quirky sense of humor could create more problems than she already had. "I just stopped to drop off your wine and pick up Baron's food, if it's come in yet?"

༄༅༄

Jonathan opened his mouth to protest Acton's arbitrary decision but left the words unsaid. A dinner stop would offer her some relief from the driving but would lengthen the trip far beyond what was safe. Nor did he want them in a situation for the handsome young doctor to offer overnight lodgings. The two of them might not have a normal romance underway, but nothing seemed normal around this woman. Why should her romances be any different? Underlying all this was an unfamiliar urge to get her to his house.

"My place is still at least three hours away," he agreed in a deliberately harsh voice. "And I doubt the rain will wait for your convenience."

Any outer evidence of exhaustion was erased by the automatic stiffening of her spine. Definitely private schools, Jonathan decided, maybe even one of the exclusive convent schools. Nowhere else could she have learned to assume the dignity of a queen so readily. Fortunately, she didn't see the amusement crossing the doctor's face at her reaction.

"No problem, Mr. Merritt," Paul broke in before she could reply. His tone was professionally soothing, no doubt the same voice he used on clients rich in money and poor in common sense. "Let me just set this wine down. Baron's food is in the storeroom." He indicated the door to Acton. She slid past, her dignity a visible mantle around her tense body. Behind her back, the look Paul shared with Jonathan was not quite as solicitous. Raised eyebrows and rolled eyes conveyed the silent equivalent of: Women!

Jonathan nodded, intrigued by the contrast between the doctor's speech and his expression, then turned away to pretend interest in a surprisingly good water-color landscape while the couple slipped through the door.

උංචං

"Are you sure you don't want to rest for a while, kiddo?" Paul's voice was muffled as he reached beyond sacks of dog food.

"You know how I am when I'm traveling. If I stop now, I won't get my body moving for days. I'll be fine. Give me that." She reached for the bag he had dragged forward.

"Not hardly. Every protective masculine instinct I don't possess has been activated. What's going on here?"

"Mr. Merritt did not approve of my review."

51

"You did accuse him of, 'Seducing the virgin wilderness and bringing it to screaming fulfillment,' or something like that, didn't you?"

"Something very vaguely like that," she admitted, with a pained frown at his inexact memory. "Still, it was meant to be a complimentary piece of writing. I don't really know why he has to go high order over it."

"Beth, I read the article, even if I can't quote it to your satisfaction. It wasn't a tepid piece of writing." Paul sounded unusually solemn. "Now that I've met the man who 'creates images of unsurpassed depth and beauty,' I wonder if he has some subtle form of revenge in mind."

"Maybe. He came into town to throw some muscle around then told Neil he would grant an interview, which he never does, if I would provide taxi service to his place in the mountains, and stay there with him. Neil thinks it's a great idea, of course."

Paul peered closely at her. No doubt he was comparing her standard casual appearance to Merritt's unconscious elegance. Bethany had always known Paul appreciated her more for her friendship than her looks.

52

Then her friend smiled, suddenly and rather wickedly.

"What do you think, kiddo?"

"I think he takes real pretty pictures."

⸙⸙⸙

They'd made the turn off the interstate an hour before and were proceeding along a roughly paved road at a speed in keeping with the darkness and the intermittent rain. Warren Zevon was calling for "Lawyers, Guns and Money" from the tape player and Jonathan was doubting he could stay awake much longer without conversation.

Acton's attention remained on the road, one hand holding the edge of the steering wheel, the other draped over the top. He wondered if she intended to spend the next two weeks in silence when she cleared her throat, shifting suddenly in her seat and scrubbing a hand across her face, muttering under her breath.

"Could you grab me a drink, Mr. Merritt? Something cold with bubbles and caffeine."

He got both of them drinks, sliding the glasses into holders on the engine cover, and decided to initiate conversation.

"It's unusual to hear Zevon these days. Did your family play eclectic music?"

"My musical tastes were developed after I left my family," she said in a tone that did not encourage further questioning.

"Why does Neil Chandler call you Acton?" He was nothing if not stubborn.

"Because it's my name."

"Then, what does BL stand for?"

"The initials I use in my by-line, which is all you need to know about." Her voice had become suddenly remote; he could almost hear the gates slam shut between them.

She didn't know how wrong she was. He was discovering that what her initials stood for was only a minuscule part of what he needed to know about her. He wanted to know how she could transfer from a confused misfit to an ice princess in faded denim with no effort. He wanted to know why she found it necessary to guard herself that way, like a child's intricate toy—dolls inside of dolls. In particular, he wanted to know why he cared, why for the first time in years he felt more than a remote interest in another person.

"Paul doesn't call you Acton."

"Paul and I have a special deal. He takes care of Baron, and I take care of the women who want to take care of him." She caught his puzzled look. "Paul is an attractive man with a successful practice, and he's single. Some women feel that's a crime against nature. When he can't discourage them, he brings me in as backup."

"And does he reciprocate?"

"That's hardly humorous, Mr. Merritt," she said quietly. "It's not as though I have to beat men off with a stick."

He realized she was serious. Did she actually believe her concealing outfits and macho attitude fooled any male with good enough eyesight to drive? He tucked away her lack of vanity to think about later. For the moment she didn't seem to be in any shape for an intense discussion.

"Would you like me to spell you driving?" he asked cautiously, not wanting to offend but not liking the way she frowned at the road.

"I've been tired before, Mr. Merritt. Don't worry, I won't—*Damn it!*"

They had rounded a corner in the suddenly increasing downpour. A young deer stood in the middle of the road, mesmerized by the headlights.

There was no time for conscious decision. Dimming her lights, she wrenched the camper toward the side of the road behind the deer, holding on with all her strength and fighting the tendency to fishtail. Released from the hypnotic effect of the light the deer bounded away unharmed, not bothering to look back as the camper slid inevitably into a shallow, muddy ditch.

CHAPTER 3

Sounds were the first thing that came back to Bethany—rain against her window, louder now that they were not moving; the ping of a cooling engine; Baron grumbling a bit as he resettled himself. Then the snick of a released seat belt, and a soft footstep before long fingers slid behind her head, lifting it away from the window frame, feeling for injuries. Warm breath flowed over her cheek, oddly comforting, and the next sound was a question in a tense, deep voice.

"Acton...BL...whatever the hell your name is. Are you all right?"

The hands behind her head and breath against her face crowded her. She stiffened, pulling away, but the fingers braced, protecting her from further damage. They cradled her head and neck, warmly supporting her while the seat belt slid across her body.

No longer able to avoid the situation she opened her eyes, meeting the assessing blue gaze in a face that seemed taut with worry. For her? Doubtful. More than likely he was concerned about his ride. Gathering her strength she straightened, and the disturbing fingers slid to her shoulders, then completely away when she shrugged.

"I'm fine, Mr. Merritt. Give me a minute to check the rig and I'll have us back on the road."

His hands reached out again as, without further discussion, she opened the driver's door and stepped out into the wet night. A low voiced exclamation, which could well have been a curse, was cut off when she slammed the door.

Going outside without her poncho was a mistake, she realized as soon as she stepped away from the vehicle's meager shelter. The rain came down with a vengeance. Wind buffeted her, driving cold dampness through layers of jacket, sweater, shirt, and undershirt. Nor was her cap any protection. Before she rounded the front of the motorhome, rain was seeping into the thick coil of her hair and running down her neck.

All this was forgotten when she slid into the bottom of the ditch. Ignoring the water washing over her sturdy hiking shoes, she braced a hand on the hood and leaned down to assess the situation. The front tire lowest in the ditch had sprouted an accessory metal pole through one wall and rested on its rim in the muddy rushing water. She bent over to take a closer look, hoping it was merely a side effect of exhaustion and incipient hypothermia. But the tire was irreparable.

"Damn, damn, damn." She punctuated each muttered curse with a fist pounding on the hood. This act had no effect on the steel, but did a good job of bruising the side of her hand.

"Problems?" The question was asked mildly.

She jumped. She'd been so involved in cursing her luck, she hadn't heard the door open. Naturally, he'd taken the time to put on a leather jacket and find a powerful flashlight. It was surprising he hadn't also found an umbrella, to keep the dampness off his thick, dark hair.

"Nothing a new tire wouldn't fix."

"You have a spare, don't you?"

"Of course I have a spare." Shocked by the thin quality of her voice, she paused, gathering strength. "It may have slipped your notice, Mr. Merritt, but it's raining. It's getting very dark and I'm very tired. Even if I had the tire changed tonight, we wouldn't be able to go on."

"My place is a little more than an hour further on. Surely we can make it that far." He sounded more puzzled than aggravated.

"The tire will have to be changed by road service. I will not travel away from town without a spare tire," she said slowly, so that he would understand. "There are no towns between here and your house and I am not about to go traipsing around strange country roads in the dark with no spare. That's *if* the road service will come tonight."

How stupid could the man be? It was obvious they were stuck until she could get the tire changed. The rain showed no sign of letting up. Even if she were able to change the tire herself, it was hours back to any town and she didn't think she could drive more than a few feet.

She had to get the motorhome into a level position before they could stop for the night. It never occurred to her to ask him for help, nor would she accept help if he offered. Long before, she learned that one helped oneself. It was safer that way. Debts had a way of demanding repayment.

"I'll have to back into that byway up there. You might as well get in out of the rain, Mr. Merritt. We can't have you getting sick."

"You're the one who should worry." Merritt raised his voice to be heard above the rain. "You're chilled and well on your way to being exhausted. It's no wonder we went off the road."

"We went off the road to avoid hitting a deer."

"Being tired reduces one's reaction time."

"I suppose you could have done it better, Mr. J. Perfect Merritt?"

※※※

Jonathan tensed, preparing for a fight, then looked more closely at her. In the harsh, reflected light, her skin had a bluish tinge and those full lips were definitely quivering, whether with cold or stress it was hard to say. Obviously BL Acton had lost control of the situation, and it scared her. Scared, she had turned like a cornered cat and fought back.

He didn't dare reach out. It would be too tempting to try to warm her lips with his tongue. A few minutes of their bodies fused together and he wouldn't notice an ark floating past. But this was not the time for thoughts of that nature. Nor did he think his tongue would remain intact if it strayed too close to her mouth. At least the cold rain helped him control his body's reaction to her.

"As a matter of fact, no, I don't think I could have done it better," he said. "The deer got away and if it hadn't been for that post, there would have been no ill effects whatsoever. Dimming your lights was a clever idea."

She glanced at him suspiciously, swiping a hand across her saturated cap before responding.

"Someone I interviewed suggested that. The first time I had a close encounter of the deer kind, I wasn't so lucky." A shudder ripped through her body and she leaned against the hood, probably seeking warmth. "I was alone, and the deer didn't die right away."

This time he did reach out, to cup her shoulder briefly, releasing her and stepping away before she could object.

He turned the flashlight on the road behind them. "The sooner we're out of this water and on level ground, the sooner we can get some rest. I'll light the way for you."

❧❧❧

With the flashlight prompting her, Bethany backed smoothly out of the ditch. Rolling unevenly due to the ruined tire, the motorhome limped backward to nestle against a gate that had not been opened for many seasons, judging by the overgrown blackberry bushes.

After she called the road service and learned they couldn't come out until the next morning, nothing more could be done that evening. Once she'd taken Baron out for a brief visit to the surrounding bushes, she could find no further excuse to avoid following him into the cozy warmth. Merritt turned as she came in, damp spots darkening the blue of his linen shirt. His leather jacket draped over the back of the passenger seat, a towel thrown over it. This was offered to her to dry Baron, and for a few moments longer she avoided eye contact while she fussed over her dog.

Eventually the setter was comfortable on his pillow under the table, a bowl of kibble in front of him, obviously not planning to move any time soon. She straightened, bracing herself to meet those cool blue eyes, but saw only his back as he busied himself in her cupboards.

"What in the world are you doing?"

"You might be able to live on air, but I have found very little nourishment in eating my words."

The look accompanying this wry statement was so self-denigrating she felt a corner of her mouth twitch.

"There's some soup and crackers. Coffee's—"

"I'm not a total loss as a traveling companion. You go dry yourself off and I'll throw something together for us."

The something was canned soup, but he added extra vegetables and some spices she'd forgotten were in the cupboards. By the time she emerged from the bathroom, dried off and warmer in a baggy navy blue sweat suit, the atmosphere in the small motorhome was rich with enticing odors. Fresh coffee waited for her next to a large bowl of soup and a basket of warmed pita bread. She hesitated. Realizing how much had gone on since she bought the bread that morning brought on a wave of exhaustion.

Before she could stagger, Merritt was there, a hand near her elbow, steadying her while she slid onto the bench seat. He stepped away promptly, resuming his seat across the small table. Subtly shifting to avoid contact between their knees, she picked up her spoon with a trembling hand. Her hand soon steadied, however, as her body received the warmth and nourishment it so desperately needed.

૯৲৩৲৩

Jonathan had learned his lesson about this woman and incautious conversation at meal times. He applied himself to his own soup in silence, finishing first and pushing the empty bowl to one side. Leaning back in the confining bench seat, he sipped at his coffee while studying her.

Her hair was still confined, this time in a thick dark towel no doubt being used to absorb moisture. It also emphasized the exhausted paleness of her skin. She had on another outfit that did nothing but encourage his curiosity. He reached for the coffee pot, ruthlessly suppressing his thoughts. His companion had obvious and very real apprehensions about him. If he ever wanted to calm her suspicions, he would have to exert more control over himself than he ever had before. He did not choose, at that moment, to wonder why he was worrying about any of this.

"This table makes into a sort of bed." She spoke into the oddly comfortable silence with ruthless efficiency. "Casey's used it once or twice, but he brings a sleeping bag. My bag's at the cleaners, I only use it in the winter..."

A fleeting touch on her arm, as he refilled her coffee, prompted a tense shrinking of her body, stopping her wandering monologue.

"There's no real problem. I'm sure I'll be comfortable."

"You don't understand," she said with a determined set to her chin. "The heater isn't working. I only have bedding for the overhead. It's dangerous to leave the oven on all night for heat, especially when you're too tired to sit up with it. Once we stop moving around and the residual heat leaks out, this place gets cold real fast."

He studied her troubled features before venturing the next question, knowing it had to be carefully worded. He wasn't aided by the fact that he faced the front of the motorhome and the snug intimacy of the bed above the driver's seat.

"So, what are the options?"

She found something fascinating to stare at in the paneling above the stove.

"You could use the overhead, and I could sleep down here with Baron. He gives off a lot of heat."

In deference to the fragility of the moment, he decided not to mention he probably put off far more heat than a dog, and over a larger area. Instead he tilted his head, taking in the bruised look below her eyes and stress lines around her mouth.

"You need a good sleep even more than I do. I'm not about to put you out of your bed."

The only solution was obvious, but he wouldn't be the one to bring it up. When the suggestion did come, it was not phrased in terms he would have preferred.

"This is stupid. There's one available bed and two of us. The bed is large enough. Unless you're claustrophobic, I'll take the outside. I'm less likely to turn the wrong way in my sleep and roll out."

It was all said in a very matter of fact, bracing fashion. Only the deepening green of her eyes and tightening of that lush mouth gave her away. A remnant impulse of the man he had almost become betrayed him before he could restrain it.

"Would it be appropriate to say I would be honored and delighted to share your bed?"

"Not hardly," she said coolly, but the look she flashed him held as much fright as anger. Bleak misery once more settled in the mossy green of her eyes. He cursed his careless impulse.

"I must apologize for that, it was needless-ly crude. I seem to be living down to your image of me."

This time she couldn't conceal her shock and he smiled slightly as he rose, turning to put his dishes into the sink and hide his relief that she had accepted his apology rather than exploding. Her deep red hair and prior reactions hinted at far greater passion than she allowed herself to reveal.

When she did blow up it could be awesome, something he looked forward to with anticipation. However, a graphic demonstration at the end of a long day could presage an even longer, colder night.

Rather than press his luck, he leaned over silently to remove his shoes. When his hands reached for his belt, he caught another flash of anxiety. This time it was more difficult to contain his impatience.

"Don't get yourself in a sweat. I just want to take my belt off so the buckle doesn't cut into me."

She flushed slightly, attempting to hide her reaction by rising and pushing past him to maneuver the overhead bed into position. This provided an excellent view of her enticingly full derriere. Jonathan swallowed past the lump in his throat, knowing there would be another lump rising further down if he didn't restrain his imagination.

This reaction wasn't normal for him. Once past adolescent foolishness he'd always been able to control his desire. By the time she was finished throwing dark paisley patterned covers over the bed, he was conveniently busy at the sink.

"You don't need to do those," she said, the cultured tones of her voice blurred by a need for rest.

"No problem." He looked over his shoulder, grinning briefly in her direction. "My mother always believed in people cleaning up their own messes. Unless you have some deep seated phobia about other people washing your dishes for you?"

∽∾∽∾

In the weak light he seemed dangerously endearing, not at all like an aggressive steam roller male. Like this, he was not a person she could easily ignore. She shrugged, striving to imply casual disinterest, and brushed past him once more, to disappear into the bathroom. "Suit yourself. I'll be a couple minutes more. You go ahead and get settled."

It was close to fifteen minutes later before she ventured into the darkened motorhome. Her unwanted guest was nothing but a large shape well to the back of the bed, and Baron had already made the jump to his accustomed spot at the foot of the sleeping area. Pausing only to flip off the small light left on to guide her, she scrambled onto the firm, familiar surface.

By great effort, she managed to ignore what was not familiar. Such as deep, even breathing from the other side of the bed. Or covers invitingly turned back for her, and pillows nested together for her head to rest on. And there did seem to be more warmth than normal in the cozy cubicle formed by closing the curtain.

Baron nestled behind her legs, conveniently separating her from the bed's other occupant. She had never spent the full night with someone else in her bed. What she had done, or what had been done to her, was not something she wanted to remember. Sleep would be impossible with another person in the bed, but at least she would be able to rest for a while. That was her last thought as she pulled the covers around herself, laid her head on the pillow and instantly fell asleep.

CCCC

Warm. She was so very warm, all the way down to her bones and nerve endings that hadn't realized how cold they were. She was surrounded by warmth and peace, dispelling the dark thoughts that were always with her. She stirred, eyes slitting open to near total darkness. Rain fell a few feet above her head, lulling her back to sleep. Baron pressed against the front of her legs and she obligingly shifted further back, nestling into incredible warmth.

It wasn't a familiar feeling, all this warmth and comfort. Doubtless this was a vivid sort of dream. It felt so very good. A breath whispered against her ear, magic words telling her to go back to sleep, to relax, that every-thing would be alright.

When she was awake, she would know better than to believe mere words. This was a dream world which encouraged forgotten fantasies of hope and comfort. Trusting for the first time in years, she nestled into the warmth and gave herself up to the fantasy.

∽∾∽

She rested against him like a half wild thing exhausted from the hunt. Jonathan cautiously eased her back another fraction of an inch, until she settled against his chest, and her sweet smelling head, under the disguising scarf, nestled under his chin. He was careful not to bring their lower bodies into contact. Any unconscious trust she might have in him would be quickly lost if she were to feel what effect her closeness was having on him.

He'd awakened to the sound of muted cries. She'd been stirring restlessly, not enough to wake herself but enough to draw his attention. The sad, lonely sounds cut through him to an area of his heart he hadn't known existed. He'd reached for her with an instinctive need to comfort, murmuring in her ear.

Whatever her demons, his whispered words seemed to dispel them. She felt so good against him, he had no wish to let her go once she was asleep again.

She needed rest and care so desperately. All day long he'd watched as the purple shadows deepened below her marvelous eyes. When she was awake, she refused all aid, her need to remain self-reliant poignantly obvious. He suspected that somewhere along the way, someone had done a masterful job of wounding the psyche of this complex, fascinating woman until she was afraid of her own femininity. There was a time once when he would have been capable of such an action himself.

Perhaps her exhaustion was caused by an evening of revelry with another man, with her stubborn refusal to allow him to help adding to the strain. Even so, he felt guilty for pressuring her into leaving with no time to prepare. Looking back, his motives, to get her by herself and teach her manners had been at best juvenile. For now he would give her the gift of a few more hours of sleep and the illusion of sanctuary, offering her the comfort of his presence when she was too tired to refuse it. There might be hell to pay in the morning but that would be a small price for the pleasure of having her rest, however briefly, against him.

∾∾∾

Bethany woke to the lack of sound. Soft early morning light filtered through the curtain. Baron leaned against the front of her knees, a note of question issuing from his throat. She felt more rested than she had in years, the half-wakened sense of euphoria so wonderful, she dreaded coming fully awake. Smiling at her insistent red dog she stretched, mentally reviewing the events of the day before to detect the source of such a feeling of well-being.

Her stretch was blocked by the solid weight of a lean thigh, snuggled against her lower body. For the first time she was aware of a hand inserted between her sweat top and undershirt, resting just below the weight of her unbound breast.

Her automatic response was one of panic. Stifling a scream, she pulled away, nearly falling out of the bunk. A move on his part to hold her brought further terror. She clawed the curtain open, scrambling until her feet were on the couch, bringing half the covers with her.

∽∾∽∾

Jonathan—snatched rudely from an erotic dream—spoke without heed, thinking with his glands rather than his mind. "For Crissakes, nothing to get into a panic about. It's not like there's anything to feel. You're all wrapped up like a sack of potatoes."

It was definitely the wrong thing to say. From blind panic and deep-rooted fear she slid straight into outright rage, obviously fueled by embarrassment at his disparagement of her feminine qualities.

"You certainly seemed eager enough to mash those potatoes a few minutes ago, Mr. Merritt. Perhaps you can find some other outlet for your energies while road service takes care of the tire. The sooner we get under way and get this farce over with, the happier I'll be." She let herself and her dog out into the bright morning.

"Way to go, lover boy," Jonathan muttered to himself, falling back among the disarranged bedding and willing his body to regain a state of sanity. It was difficult to calculate how much this had increased her hostility, but he had a feeling it was to geometric proportions. He grinned ruefully, remembering what a difference blazing fury made in her appearance.

Danger to his more delicate body parts notwithstanding, he found himself preferring the outraged fire breathing Amazon to the elegant ice princess. He rubbed his palm along his now relaxed thigh, wondering how much worse it would have been if he had not, even in his sleep, been aware of her every movement.

His hand cupped again, remembering soft womanly flesh nestled in his palm. She felt so right cuddled trustingly against his body. Then he reminded himself that memories were all he would have if he didn't get moving.

CHAPTER 4

It was easy to see how J. Phillip Merritt would be able to take spectacular nature photos, Bethany decided. If she lived among such a proliferation of wildlife beauty, the problem would have been setting the camera down long enough to fix meals or change film. Then again, as she knew from her own experience, proximity to magnificent vistas did not automatically make one a magnificent photographer.

All this went through her head in an early-morning-after-a-late-night idle fashion as she waited for Baron to quit sniffing around and follow her indoors. He was testing the rich pine-scented air, trying to entice her into letting him run free as he was sure he was meant to do.

"No way, kiddo. Not until we find out the ground rules. If we have to spend the next few days in the august company of Mr. J. Phillip

Merritt, we're going to make our lives as painless as possible."

She encouraged the setter up rough wood and stone steps into the cabin that was a masterpiece of open space design. She'd been too tired the night before to appreciate more than a bed covered in handmade quilts. That morning her eye had been drawn to wide windows framing vistas that encouraged her to follow Baron without delay.

She now followed the scent of freshly brewed coffee and other enticing aromas through the silent house to a room of open beams, copper pots, and windows facing the morning sun. Merritt was seated at a rough-hewn table tucked in a nook of windows, the sun haloing around his tousled dark hair. A flannel shirt flapped open over faded blue jeans and his feet were thrust into moccasins. Nothing could have been further from the man she had met in Neil's office. She found herself almost attracted to this facet of him.

∽∾∽

Jonathan looked up from grim contemplation of a mug of black coffee to take in her appearance. The night's rest had done wonders for her, lightening the shadows under her eyes and removing the translucent look of her skin. She was scrubbed clean and freshly dressed in a turtleneck, jungle dungarees and hiking boots. Her hair was pinned up and out of her way under a battered olive green cap.

"Good God, woman, do you sleep in those uniforms?"

The contentment on her face faded as if it had never existed. Obviously striving for control, Acton crossed the kitchen to fill a mug left out by the coffee pot. Rejecting the bench across from him, she leaned against the tile counter, crossing her free arm in front of her body. Baron sensed the tension in the atmosphere, and elected to curl up in a warm corner.

"If anyone knew the answer to that question it would be you, wouldn't it, Mr. Merritt?"

He'd hated the words as they had erupted from his mouth and despised them even more when they caused the light to go out of her face. Her defensive posture wasn't lost on him, nor did he miss the tightening of that oh-so-tempting mouth. How could he explain that mornings had never been his strong point, even less so when his night had been filled with erotic memories and even more compelling fantasies?

When he'd looked in on her the night before, she was curled on her side in a fall of moonlight. The quilts were pulled all the way up to her chin and her hair, uncovered but still loosely pinned, had been a glorious spill of softness around her tired features. Baron looked up from his chosen spot tucked in behind her legs. Jonathan could remember how her back had felt, sleek and warm against his chest even under the clothes, and found himself envying a dog. Then this morning she'd been gone, the bed made up and no evidence she'd ever been there.

Seeing her once again armored against an unfriendly world, her face alive with the beauty of the morning, he reverted to the person he had left Europe to resist becoming. He wanted to show her his woods, to be beside her for every fascinating discovery. If he didn't do something about himself, the most he would be showing her would be how to get down the mountain.

He rose and reached past Acton, ignoring her quickly concealed flinch. Opening the oven door let loose a mélange of tempting aromas, and he snagged a pot holder from the side of the stove, adroitly pulling out a tray of golden biscuits. They spilled neatly into a basket already lined with a bright gingham tea towel. Stepping around her, he gathered up plates, knives and napkins laid out on the counter and made his way back to the table.

 erxerx

Bethany stared. "You made biscuits?"

A mocking brow asked her who else there was to make them. She also interpreted it as questioning if she would have made them, or if she could. Flushing at the inanity of her question, she idled over to the sun-drenched breakfast nook, so appealingly set with earthenware dishes that matched the mugs. Butter filled a crock beaded with condensation that glistened in the early morning sun. The same sun highlighted clear jars of jelly, bathing the table in their hues of peach and purple.

She slid hesitantly onto the bench across from Merritt, whose full attention seemed to be on the steaming biscuit he was hiding under layers of butter and jelly. He didn't raise his head, but nudged the basket in her direction. She took a biscuit hesitantly, bringing it closer to her face to break it open and engulf her senses in its warm essence.

"It smells wonderful," she offered.

He indicated the crock of butter, and pushed the jelly jars closer, obviously intending her to make herself at home. Such an offer did not need to be repeated, particularly when she discovered she was ravenous. The butter melted instantly, and the jelly was diligent in offering up its goodness. She took a large bite, closing her eyes in sheer sensual enjoyment.

"Where did you learn to bake like this?"

He shrugged, appropriating another biscuit and decorating it before popping a liberal portion into his mouth, followed by a healthy swig of coffee. She couldn't stop herself from watching the action of his throat muscles, nor from imagining the path the biscuit took. From the outside, that path was well defined by dark chest hair that lessened as it tracked lower but never seemed to totally—she jerked her gaze away, wondering when it had turned so warm and striving to remember the lessons of her youth. Advanced deportment had never covered breakfasts with unshaven men who were practically bare chested and produced biscuits that could win awards.

"Did you mother teach you how to bake?" As a conversational gambit, it covered many areas. It brought in the opportunity of discussing his early life, which would be a good starting point for the interview. It also reminded him he had a mother who had instilled respect for floundering females along with the ability to cut shortening into flour.

He nodded.

She felt her temper—that distant, barely known part of her she kept segregated from her daily life—pull at its chains, demanding some time out in the world. She repressed it automatically.

"You must be excessively hungry, Mr. Merritt," she said graciously. Mademoiselle would have been so proud of her. "Perhaps you are not a morning person?"

He smiled, finally bringing his devastating sky blue morning gaze fully upon her face.

"I thought perhaps if I filled my mouth with biscuits, I might keep my foot out of it for a while."

⌒⌒⌒

She didn't laugh. It was too soon for that. She didn't even really smile. But a glow began to seep back into her face, softening parts that had been too long frozen. A slender, slightly trembling hand reached back into the biscuits.

Jonathan indulged himself for the moment, feeling a vaguely primitive thrill from watching her enjoy his food. Before she could become too aware of his scrutiny, he shifted his attention.

"Actually, Dad taught us how to make biscuits. Mom's specialty is jellies and candies."

She stopped, shocked, golden peach jam dropping from her knife onto the waiting biscuit.

"Did she make these?"

"The jellies. My sister Amy makes most of the jams."

He watched her closely now, trying to gauge from her face—one that seemed to have so much experience at remaining with-drawn—if she had the same amused contempt for "home-made" that his ex-wife Marlene had. Why did it matter, anyway?

She set down her knife, reaching for one of the half full jars. On the front was a whimsical sticker, depicting a Victorian era cook up to her elbows in work and loving it. The contents were labeled as being apple jelly, from the kitchen of "Mom" with love. She handled the jar with the reverence reserved for a Faberge egg.

"Didn't your mother ever make jelly?" he asked, his voice low, reacting to the forlorn look on her face.

She dredged up a near smile, unaware how out of place it looked on a face filled with too many sad thoughts. Then she set down the jar sharply, shaking her head.

"My mother died when I was ten. She didn't have time to make jelly." The flatness in her voice matched perfectly with the loss of her peaceful expression. "Will you be wanting to start the interview this morning, Mr. Merritt?"

He felt his past-self threatening once again to take over. She'd come so close to opening up. Drawing a steadying breath, he delayed answering by taking a sip of coffee before responding.

"There's no reason to race into it, Ms. Acton. Get to know my woods first. Then you'll be able to understand me, and your article won't contain the misconceptions that seem to be so common among writers."

"Do you feel there were misconceptions in the review?"

He set his mug down with a thud. "Later, Ms. Acton."

❧❧❧

"You know, you were wrong about this dog being harmless," Jonathan observed, untangling himself for the third time from the enthusiastic young setter's leash. "Under the right circumstances he would be classifiable as a menace. Can't he be trusted off lead?"

"The lead is for your benefit. I thought this would be a wildlife protected area."

"Any wildlife that can't stay out of the way of that clown would never make it through the winter. Would he run away?"

87

"He always comes back. Don't you, kid?" she crooned while removing both collar and leash. For a moment Baron remained close, until the significance of a dangling collar got through the sensory overload he'd been experiencing all morning. With a muffled "wuff" he was off in a flash of glossy red hair.

"You don't leave identification on him?"

"He's tattooed and has a microchip. But he's never been out of sight for more than fifteen minutes. It's the positive side of the tradeoff. I got a gorgeous animal long on affection but short on conventional smarts. Straying would take too much planning."

This startled a laugh out of him, and he gestured to a rise in front of them, careful not to encroach on her space.

"Let me show you my world, B. L. Acton."

಄಄಄

"You have a lot of wildlife that doesn't seem overly shy. Have you made it a point to be friendly with them?" Bethany asked the question carefully. So far, Merritt had avoided answering anything that sounded like the lead-in to an interview.

"Not anymore."

His abrupt response brought her attention fully centered on the man who had, for most of the day, been congenial and charming. Except for his brief early morning grumpiness, this was the man who had fixed her dinner. It was a welcome contrast to what she'd expected the visit to be like, but she wasn't sure if he was pretending to be someone he was not, or if she had misjudged him from the start.

Now he waited for her at the crest of the hill, one hip propped on a wide shelf of rock. There was ample room for her to rest next to him without feeling threatened. Baron had long since given up exploring, and was grateful for the opportunity to collapse at her feet. She sensed Merritt was about to reveal something about himself, if she would allow him time to speak in his own words. It had proven to be her most effective interviewing technique.

"When I first moved here," he continued in a pensive voice, "I was enchanted by the woods and the animals, the whole getting back to nature thing. It seemed to be a clean and simple existence and...I needed that. In spite of all the learned advice, I was determined to make friends with as many animals as possible.

"The first few years, I did a lot of supplemental feedings, and was able to get close to some of the calmer species. I was convinced it could only improve my work to have my subjects so available and cooperative." He paused, staring out at the valley that stretched below them. She didn't think he saw the dark green of the pines or the occasional explosive orange of early changing oaks.

"We had a couple of mild winters, and the populations increased. Then I had to go to Europe late one fall, and couldn't get back here before an early blizzard. The kid who helped me from time to time had to go back to college early. By the time he could get in touch with me and I could get up here, it was too late to help some of the animals, and they'd never learned to help themselves." He pushed himself up from the boulder, standing with his back to her, his hands thrust, palms out, into the back pockets of his well-worn jeans.

"After that, I stayed out of their way. I still leave out salt blocks but the only time I offer feed is when the weather is too bad for even the good foragers to find anything."

Had it been another time, had she been another person, she would have offered comfort verbally or perhaps by laying a hand on his shoulder. As it was, she waited, considering the story against the limited amount of information available concerning this man, knowing she would never use it in an article. He'd given her the inestimable gift of his private beliefs. She knew better than most how special a gift that was.

c√3c√3

After a long pause Jonathan shook himself and continued. "Interestingly enough, when I go over my work of that time, I'm not satisfied with any of it. I don't know if my memories cloud my perceptions or if it's obvious the subjects are not truly wild. Whatever, they lack...essence." His shoulders lifted in a self-deprecatory shrug, and he turned to her with a manufactured grin ready to paste across his face.

What he saw stopped the artificial reactions. There was compassion in her mossy green eyes and more softness of her features than he'd seen before. He suspected her reaction was as much sorrow for the animals as sympathy for the hard lessons he'd learned. But he would take any emotional response he could get from her for now. If it took a few more examples of his private pain to draw out her sense of compassion, so be it. He was patient. Usually. This time, he would nurture a delicate wild creature, not destroy it.

He got to his feet. "Let's get back. I want to see if I can tempt you with my cheese and ham sandwiches."

⛤⛤

Bethany made another circuit of the kitchen and living area. Nope, not here, either. Not in her bedroom, but she wouldn't have expected that. This early in the morning, there were a few corners of the spacious living room still in shadow, but those weren't large enough to hide anything.

"Looking for something, Ms. Acton?" The voice was gruff with just-wakened impatience.

Merritt, of course. She groaned to herself. Of all things—to be found poking through his house, less than two days after her arrival. Straightening slowly she turned, offering him a placating smile while hoping he would be at least partially dressed.

He was in the same attire as the morning before: jeans, an open shirt, and moccasins on his bare feet. Why did the sight of his lean ankles disturb her so? Collecting herself, Bethany cleared her throat. Not nervously, of course, but for some reason, lately she'd been having trouble getting words out.

"Sorry to disturb you, Mr. Merritt. I was looking for your telephone." She made a useless gesture with one of her hands to indicate the failure of her search. "I need to check in before everyone gets wrapped up in something else."

Merritt rubbed a hand over his face then looked around the room, as though trying to remember where he had left the phone.

"Why? They know where you are."

"I need to see if Neil will let Casey get pictures of some of the women who were helped by that shelter. That way, I won't have to wait on him when I get a chance to talk to them myself."

Scowling, Merritt rested his hands on his hips. Clever hands with long fingers rested on age-whitened jeans that fit comfortably low on those lean hips. His shirt opened, displaying more of a lean-muscled chest, lightly sprinkled with dark hair, than she had seen the day before. Bethany cleared her throat again and forced herself to look away. Why was a partially clothed body so much more enticing than one totally naked? Or did the body itself make a difference? She wasn't sure she wanted to know.

"What's wrong with the phone in your rig? Or did you try to use it?" His voice was no less grumpy than before, though he seemed marginally more awake.

How many times could she clear her throat without sounding like a total blithering idiot? "It doesn't seem to be working," she admitted trying not to sound too utterly hopeless.

"You did try turning it on first, didn't you?"

"I understand how to use the stupid thing, even if I don't like it." She peered at him closely. His attitude seemed extremely surly, almost like the morning before, and also in her motorhome. "You don't like mornings, do you?"

He shuddered visibly, pushing his hand through thick, sleep-roughened dark hair. "Lord, no. I had to get up early every morning until I left home. As far as I'm concerned, life shouldn't start until well after the first two cups of coffee." He looked over at her, obviously seeing the laughter she was trying to hide. "I suppose you like mornings."

"Love them," she admitted with what she hoped was a conciliatory smile. "It's the freshest time of day, even in the cities. I learned to appreciate mornings when I was growing up." She'd appreciated them even more later, when it was the only time she could have almost to herself. Just another one of those things she no longer thought about. "How in the world do you get such marvelous sunrise shots when you hate mornings?"

Now he seemed almost contrite, as though his manners had finally caught up with his awakening mind. "I generally stay up all night. Somehow, it doesn't seem as much like morning then." He drew a deep breath, rubbing his chest. As though realizing for the first time his chest was bare, he began to button his shirt. "Thank you, by the way. Have you checked your plug?"

She tore her attention away from the chest now being covered. Even though her mind generally worked very well in the mornings, he had just totally lost her.

"Could you repeat that please?"

He looked up, frowning slightly, then seemed to remember his last words. "Thank you, for your comment about the sunrise shots. Have you checked the connecting plug on your mobile phone?"

"I think Neil had it wired directly when he found out I was likely to unplug it unless I absolutely had to call someone."

"Why in the world do you have the damned thing?"

She shrugged, turning away to enjoy the view through the large window. It was bright enough now to see the closer, individual trees and some of the bushes along the edge of the clearing.

"When I hit that deer, out in the desert?" Out of the corner of her eye, she saw him moving closer. He nodded, obviously remembering their previous conversation. "I messed up my tire. I had used up my spare earlier that week and didn't get around to replacing it."

"Which explains why you were bothered on the way up here," he commented, as though confirming an earlier thought.

"I suppose. Anyway, I had no way to get in touch with anyone until a rancher came by, much later, who was able to call for some help. When Neil found out he had the phone put in. He said it made Marsha worry less about me."

"But you still hate it."

"It's intrusive. I'd rather just pick up messages along the way. If I wanted people to be able to bother me all the time, I'd live in one spot."

"Makes sense to me." Mostly awake now, Merritt reached over to a cupboard near the entrance to the hall. It opened to reveal a small cubicle, complete with telephone, fax machine and an answering machine that was blinking helplessly. He pushed a couple of buttons then lifted the receiver, holding it briefly to his ear. "Use this for now. I'll get some coffee going and take a look at your mobile later."

"What about your messages?" She looked at the now dark button with something akin to loathing. She had never gotten used to the artificial personality of answering machines.

He hesitated on the way to the kitchen then shrugged. "My agent uses the fax and my family e-mails. The only people who call don't matter enough to deal with before lunch." He offered her a charmingly roguish smile, rather like a schoolboy getting away with something slightly naughty. "Hurry up. I'll get some breakfast going. Since you dragged me out at the crack of dawn, we might as well see if we can spot the golden eagles out hunting."

Receiver forgotten, Bethany stared at the spot he'd just occupied, until irritating sounds began to issue from the plastic demon in her hand. Time to work. Later, she would try to figure him out.

ℰↄℰↄ

"Look, out there. No, more to the—" As if impatient for her to look in the correct spot, Merritt stepped behind Bethany, cupping her shoulder with one hand, sliding the long fingers of his other hand along her jaw. Bending forward to bring them into the same field of vision, he shifted her until his chin, excitingly rough and fragrant with masculine scents, touched her sensitive cheek.

She turned as he guided her and was rewarded by the sight of a golden eagle riding the thermal highways through the heavy clouds. Then Merritt shifted, brushing his slightly rough cheek along hers, and she lost interest in the bird.

Since they'd set out that morning, Merritt had gone out of his way to be a pleasant companion. This included some fleeting touches, mostly a casual brushing of his fingers when he was pointing something out or encouraging her to precede him along the trail. These seemed to follow the natural order of their walk and were certainly nothing to become upset about.

Now, she was feeling hemmed in, held between his strong fingers and warm cheek, with the added intimacy of his breath feathering against her face. It could have been innocent, nothing more than the desire to show her the eagle. But she felt again that strange stirring, a yearning deep inside that became more apparent to her the longer she was around this man.

Ten years before she'd locked this feeling away. She'd learned the hard way that any lack of control gave others too much power over her. It was a lesson she wasn't likely to forget. She stiffened, pulling away from him.

Before she could do much more than start to lean away he stepped to one side, casually reaching for the camera that seemed an appendage to his body. The whirr-click of the camera motor helped to fill the suddenly awkward silence.

"Another fabulous Merritt photograph to thrill your public?" she asked, the sharpness in her voice disguising the shakiness.

"Perhaps. It could also be another roll of pictures of a bird flying around." Apparently, he chose to remain calm in the face of her derision "I know how it seems the photo will come out, but it can fool me, sometimes positively, sometimes negatively.

"There was a time," she began, almost apologetically, "when I thought to follow in the footsteps of the great photographers." While she spoke, she didn't look directly at him but stared over the valley, contemplating the relative freedom of the eagle and all the wild things. Gathering rain clouds, supported by pillars of sunlight, covered the sky. "I remember thinking how wonderful it would be to travel around and take pictures of where I'd been, beautiful photographs other people would want to buy from me. I had sufficient opportunity and a decent camera. Somehow, instead of my pictures being worth a thousand words, I found myself needing a thousand words to explain the pictures."

⁊ɔ⁊ɔ

Jonathan did not interrupt her, did not dare even to look at her. Her voice, so rich in nuances, so very soothing, eased over him like warm honey. He'd never before heard anyone discuss their failed goals so honestly.

"Finally, one of the magazines I sent pictures to suggested I give up on the illustrations and concentrate on writing articles. But I was determined to be a photographer. Shortly after that, I met someone *Western Living* had been trying to interview for years. Instead of sending photos with lengthy captions, I sent in a full length article with illustrations. Neil asked for a re-write, bought the article, and sent out a staff photographer. Thus ended my career as a photographer."

He wanted to grab her up and hold her in an excess of emotions shared and understood, of life secrets entrusted. But it was too soon. It might always be too soon. He willed himself not to react unduly to the gentle whimsy and honest self-evaluation of this remarkable woman. An all too fleeting brush of his palm over her shoulder produced the by now familiar sweet shock of recognition.

"Thus started said career as a writer. I've seen those thousand words, BL Acton. You have an advantage I will never have. I have to wait for the perfect sunset and attempt to capture it on film. You can create it out of your own mind and imagination. Never belittle your ability with words. It is a gift— and a reward for all your hard work."

She had no answer for that, only rose-tinged cheeks and a near smile thrown more or less in his direction. He waited, wondering how often she received compliments, and if they always made her nervous. What effect would his next question have on her?

"Which is why I've been wondering, these past few days, why you squander yourself as you do."

The gentle glow disappeared in a wave of fiery ice. The color she showed in her cheeks had nothing to do with shyness and everything to do with outrage. "What exactly do you mean by that?"

"You're a highly talented writer with an unusual ability to communicate with people who would prefer you not bother them. You could be interviewing heads of state, people of world importance, yet you limit yourself to atypical people who are so far out of touch with society they are no threat to your goal of avoiding life."

"I do my job well. What business is it of yours who I interview?"

"I've seen waste too often and not said anything about it. It disturbs me to stand by and watch you squander your ability on such trivial subjects." As he spoke, he unconsciously reached out to her, trying to communicate his sincerity by touch as well as words.

"Present company included, Mr. Merritt?" she swerved, adroitly avoiding his hand. "Maybe I'm just wasting my 'talent' here as well as my time."

Before he could step forward she'd whirled and was running away from him, back down the trail, as the threatening clouds finally began to drop rain in huge splotches. Very soon, the rocks would become dangerously slippery. Muttering a curse at himself, he hurried after her.

CHAPTER 5

The rain cooled her cheeks as Bethany navigated the trail far more quickly than was wise. She knew it would be only a matter of time before he caught up with her; his woodsman-ship was far superior to her own. Fleeing had been an automatic reaction. Rationally, she knew he hadn't meant to insult her, nor could she form a valid argument against his observations. But the abrupt tone and blunt phrasing had come as a shock after the innocuous, bland conversation.

He caught up to her as she was slowing, having realized Baron wasn't at her side. Without a word he grasped her arm, steadying her and hurrying through the increasing downpour. They made it as far as a heavy stand of pine before the sky opened up and dumped on them. Merritt ducked under an overhang of ancient granite, pulling her with him.

It was a confined space, and their combined body heat soon dispelled some of her chill, making her even more aware of his presence. She stiffened, thinking to pull away. In an automatic gesture he grabbed her other arm, holding her steady. She quickly lost any semblance of relaxation.

"Take it easy." He didn't let go, but did ease the strong bite of his fingers. "Look, I'm sorry. I realize I have no right to comment on your choice of a career."

"No, you don't have that right." There was anger in her voice, not panic. The panic would come if he didn't back away.

"I've given you the right to pry into my life and expose it because I believe in your ability to put words together. I also believe you are far better than you give yourself credit for." His fingers moved against her arms, subtly stroking. She felt the beginning of a flush of warmth along her skin and attempted again to pull away.

"Mr. Merritt, if you please," she muttered, intentionally formal.

"You know, Acton," he began, his voice sober, "anyone listening to us would think they'd been transported back a couple of generations." His grip eased but his hands remained on her arms, holding her in front of him. "You insist on addressing me like some pompous Victorian gentleman. All I can address you by is your by-line and every time we talk about something other than trees or birds you shut me out. And by the way, my name is Jonathan, BL Acton. I would appreciate it if you would use it."

The seeming non-sequitur, delivered in the same schoolmaster voice, brought a tiny, reluctant grin to her face. He'd kept her so off balance the last few days, nothing surprised her much anymore, not even the fact that she wasn't annoyed by his appraisal of her life's work.

Bethany looked out at the curtain of rain and sighed. "I can't stay mad at you when I wonder myself how long I can enjoy curmudgeon hunting. It was fun in the beginning but lately I feel like I'm missing something."

"Would that have anything to do with BL Acton's review of my book?"

"I think it might. I'd never written anything quite like that before."

"You mean you never said someone's 'most recent offering to an unworthy public is a sensuous affirmation of this man's love affair with nature'?" He quoted the words precisely, an unholy gleam lighting his eyes.

"Not hardly." She tried to speak dryly and restrain her wayward tongue. But control had been lost, somewhere on the trip to this mountain retreat. As though the winding road had been a passage to a very special, almost magical place. "At least, not that anyone's ever seen."

"Then I am truly honored, Ms. Acton."

She stood within the constraint of his hands, her body very still but no longer tensed for flight. There was a fresh new feel to the woods, a forest smell of new life that would be developing below the ground during the coming winter, ready to surprise the world after the snow melted.

"Bethany," she said, looking out at sunlight filtering between drops of rain that fell inches in front of her face. She felt his body shift, his fingers tighten slightly as he bent his head to see her averted face more clearly. She dared to lift her chin, looking him fully in the eyes. "My mother named me Bethany."

ഇരെ

Bethany. Her name conjured up images of a time long past when women had romantic names and heart-breakingly delicate faces, with voices created to form soft words that drove a man crazy. It was anachronistic, as unusual and unconsciously romantic as she was. He had never known anyone with the name, and he couldn't think of any name that would suit her better. Reacting as much to the yearning message in her eyes as to the gift of her name, Jonathan edged closer, sliding his hands up to cup her shoulders.

Before she could protest, before she could remind him she was there to interview him, not entertain him, he was stopped by an influx of wet dog, the storm, and his own better judgment.

Whining and shuddering, Baron forced his soggy body between their legs, vigorously relieving himself of surface moisture. In the process he completely did away with any of the sheltering benefits of the small overhang. Clinging to his dignity by a supreme effort, Jonathan managed a slight bow.

"I am honored to make your acquaintance, Miss Bethany. May I now suggest we get the hell out of here before your mutt manages to drown us?"

They didn't run off hand in hand, but there was much shared emotion during the dash through trees and rain. Jonathan urged Bethany ahead of him. More than a gallant gesture, it gave him time to remind himself that all she had offered was her name. Not the increasingly appealing body on the trail ahead of him. He vowed to himself, no matter what followed, Bethany Acton would not be sorry she had become his friend.

⁊⁊⁊

"I built that fire to keep you warm. It would be nice if you could manage to take advantage of it."

The impatient voice jerked Bethany erect, pulling her away from the half-dozing state she'd slid into while tending Baron. Apparently the setter had attempted to forge a new path through berry bushes that afternoon. Bitter experience had taught her she'd have to cut the brambles out of Baron's silky coat if she didn't comb him out completely before he dried.

Now that she was forcibly reminded, she felt the chill of damp clothing against her body. This could be ignored, as she had in the past. What she could not ignore was the lean strength of the fingers taking a firm hold of her shoulders, pulling her closer to the fire. She looked up and, for just an instant, memories overshadowed his silhouette. Reason prevailed, and she shifted.

"You're still soaked. Here, at least drink some of this."

She accepted the proffered coffee with a slight smile, sipped gratefully before putting it down on the hearth beside her. The mug was almost hot against her fingers. Was she really that cold?

"It will do more good inside you than in the mug. Take a break. If you're only half as wet as I was, steam's going to be rising from your back."

"In a minute," she agreed absently. "He has a spot here..." She bent closer to the profusely feathered red ears, working a wide toothed comb gently through the hair, dislodging bits of debris with every cautious stroke. She jumped when Jonathan's hand passed over her head, removing the cap.

"You have a spot here, and all over your body. Leave Baron alone for a minute. Being damp won't kill a dog."

Bethany clapped a hand to her head, fingers grazing the soaked cap as it was pulled away. She reached but stopped when the cap was tossed casually aside to lay in a small sodden heap on a pile of damp towels. He dropped a dry towel on her snugly pinned-up hair.

"Here, Sister Bethany, if it bothers you so much to go around with your head bare."

She flinched, then grabbed for the towel as it began to slide off her head. He stepped away, running a hand roughly through his own hair. It was as though they were back at the beginning, sniping at each other for no good reason, with her jumping at every sudden move. She heard him curse under his breath, then he dropped his thick sweater into her lap.

"Here," Jonathan shouldered her gently aside. "Let me take care of this clown for you while you try to take care of yourself."

Bethany hesitated, at a loss how to respond. No one had ever taken care of Baron for her before. Then again, no one had tried to take care of her for years. It was unsettling. Not necessarily bad, just unsettling. She edged off the quilt set near the comforting warmth of the fire, reluctant to change in his presence but knowing she had to get at least her sodden outer layers off before she became chilled to the bone.

In the end she compromised by moving behind Jonathan and turning her back on him, peeling off the heavy over-shirt and clinging sweater with some difficulty. She watched over her shoulder for him to indicate any attention in her direction. But he seemed to be focusing his concentration solely on Baron, rubbing a towel along lean red sides, watching a hind leg vibrate and teeth show in an idiot's grin.

The sweater was soft and comfortable, even warmer than she had thought it would be. Perhaps she was colder than she had realized. Bethany snuggled unconsciously against the wool until she realized that the scent and warmth now surrounding her had come from his body. Flushing, she sat down near him, busying herself with turning back the drooping sleeves to free her hands so she could reach for the comb.

"It was my sister's first attempt at a full sized sweater," he said, indicating sleeves that refused to fold evenly.

"Your sister made this for you?" Panicked, she began to pull off the sweater before she remembered she had nothing to replace it with.

"Don't be ridiculous. Peggy would be thrilled to know someone was getting use out of it. She sends me a new one every year." He seemed about to say something else, then concentrated on the dozing setter, refusing to relinquish the comb.

"No, you eat something first," he ordered. "And dry your own hair. Baron's fine. You getting sick won't do him any good."

Bethany shrugged, acknowledging the truth of his statement. She swallowed some hot soup, nibbled on the corner of a sandwich and drained her coffee. A cursory pass of the towel over her hair removed some moisture. She satisfied herself with shaking out the towel and wrapping it turban style around her head before she moved back to her dog.

Baron was flipped over, waking long enough to grump about the procedure, then fell back asleep when Bethany rested his head in her lap. She sat tailor fashion by the fire, straightening her back briefly to relieve the aching, then once more bent over a particularly stubborn collection of briars.

She heard Jonathan move around the room, efficiently returning the area around the fireplace to its normal cozy condition. In spite of the image he'd first tried to convey, the time she spent in his company had shown him to be an intrinsically decent person. He still displayed occasional flashes of the man she'd met and instinctively feared in Neil's office. But that was J. Phillip Merritt, she reminded herself with a tired giggle. She was staying with Jonathan now.

Bethany caught herself, just before falling over on top of her sleeping dog. Baron was combed out and dry enough to not spread doggy odor throughout the house. Her own clothes were damp but warmed by the fire, and the hot food she'd been forced to eat helped her to re-fuel internally. Only now did she become conscious of the growing discomfort of cramping, over-exerted muscles. She wondered if she would have the strength to get up before she froze in this position for all time.

"Here, lean back against this." The low voice came just before a padded support was inserted behind her shoulders. A gentle hand enforced the command. Long, increasingly familiar fingers searched out the tension that had been building in her neck and shoulders.

The days of undemanding companionship helped her decision to relax. Shifting Baron onto the quilt, she straightened her legs and leaned back, murmuring her pleasure. The magic fingers continued their comfort, now reaching between her shoulder blades, rubbing small circles through the heavy sweater. A soft moan of blissful pleasure escaped between her barely parted lips. Bethany allowed herself to succumb to the comfort of the moment. It felt like a heaven she had not imagined in her wildest fantasies. Magic fingers took away tension, strain, exhaustion, the towel on her head, her...hairpins?

Adrenaline surged through her veins, straightening her spine away from the too enticing support. But she could not straighten away from the fingers that had somehow worked their way into her hair. They followed her panicked surge, not pulling, but also not releasing.

"Easy there. You were too busy taking care of Baron to take care of yourself, and since I don't have anything pressing to do..." His soothing voice barely ruffled the damp hair now covering her ears.

He wasn't pressuring her to lean back but he still wasn't removing his fingers from her hair. Her tired mind couldn't come up with any immediate reason to not trust him. She eased back against the hassock with her legs curled underneath her, ready in case she needed to spring away. Bethany would have had to go far back in her memory, to a time before her world had changed, to remember having felt so thoroughly comforted and at ease. Jonathan's hands worked slowly through her hair, performing a quiet, special sort of wizardry on her. For the first time in her adult memory she gave in and trusted another human being. Sighing in private ecstasy, she went boneless against the ottoman.

ↄ⁃ↄↄ⁃ↄ

It was a victory of sorts. Jonathan chose to ignore the tension in her legs and concentrate on the fact that she was allowing his fingers to slip slowly through the rich dark fire of her hair. It unraveled slowly, falling in damp swirling clumps around her shoulders. A thick, warmed, towel blotted up most of the moisture as he squeezed one section after another. Since her hair had been pinned up and protected by the scarf there were no twigs, and few tangles, to remove.

Soon it slid like the finest silk threads through his fingers, caressing the sensitive inner surfaces as he caressed her scalp. He inhaled the scent of rain and the forest and the elusive clean fragrance that was simply Bethany, a scent more compelling than the most potent of perfumes. Fanning out her hair, he began to stroke through it with the brush he'd found in her room.

"So lovely. So soft." He breathed another glancing kiss against her hair. He knew it was a danger zone, knew she could revert to panic at any minute. But now, in the twilight time of near sleep, she was delightfully mellow. Her only reaction was a slight grimace as a thick strand escaped to tickle her eyelash.

It was a golden opportunity to touch the skin he'd been secretly coveting. So gently she barely realized he'd been there, he brushed his palm against her cheek, stroking back the errant lock, bringing it to rest briefly against his own cheek.

"I'm so glad you didn't decide to cut your hair when you took on your tough reporter persona. It doesn't totally fit the facade, does it? Is that why you keep all this beauty hidden away?"

❦

Bethany heard his comments first as a soothing mutter against her scalp, a further gentling influence. Then the full import came to her as the words sank in. "Facade—Cut your hair—" Chaos attacked the ease she'd been feeling, defeating it readily. She was too busy panicking to notice.

Straightening suddenly, she pulled away from his hold, coming up onto her knees next to the ottoman. Any pain she may have felt from her unbound hair being wrenched out of his grasp was incidental. She grabbed at the unruly mass as it threatened to blind her, pulling it back at the base of her neck.

"I didn't realize how late it had gotten. So sorry. Thank you for the coffee and—

everything." She was standing now, reaching out for her damp clothes, holding them against her body like a shield. Baron rose with her, grumbling at having been disturbed. It was simple, after all, to escape. Jonathan made no comment while she was in the room, though she thought she heard an angry curse as she slipped into her lonely bedroom.

ↄ৵ↄ৵

The images developed slowly, taking on increasing depth and character as carefully mixed solutions washed over chemically sensitive paper. First the forms were revealed—slender, graceful body covered in clothing that did nothing to enhance, the glory of her hair concealed. At her feet, at her side, leaping up to her face was the loyal clown friend, the only creature lucky enough to have her continuing company.

They played, rested, contemplated, looked out, totally unaware he'd been trapping every moment, every thought, every hidden emotion with his camera and his skill. It had been the most difficult project of his career, and the most rewarding. First, he established trust with these wild, fey creatures. They'd become accustomed to his presence to such an extent they forgot for long periods of time he was there, the camera an appropriate appendage to his hand and eye. The results were almost an invasion of privacy, revealing more about her than she would have ever wanted anyone to know.

Jonathan lifted the enlargements out one at a time, hanging them to dry while he attempted to evaluate the work. He was discovering his objectivity slipping away more every day. Every iota of trust, every furtive glance was a milestone. The easing of her wariness had come so slowly and was to be savored even more because of that.

Last night had been a mistake. He'd allowed his impatience to rule and had nearly driven her back behind the walls again. There had been a time, he remembered with a wry grimace as he moved more photos from one tray to the next, when he never miscalculated with members of the opposite sex. He'd attained a reputation for always knowing the right thing to say and do with every woman. Now, when it was so critically important, he seemed to be ruled more by his glands than at any time since his freshman year in college.

Away from home for the first time, he had cut a swath through the coeds a mile wide. It was fortunate that had been a time when the extreme dangers of promiscuity were far in the future. They all acted like the healthy, curious young animals they were. What happened later, after he left college, was another matter, one he had not thought of for a long time. He thought he'd put all that behind him, only to find the memories encroaching more and more of late.

Idly, Jonathan wondered how much having Bethany around influenced his recent restless memories. Was it because she obviously had ghosts of her own locked inside herself? Some of those ghosts had emerged the night before, to take away the comfort and ease growing between them. Although he cursed at the time, he had to admit she provided a very necessary slowing to the way events were progressing. As long as the mistrust wouldn't be a long term situation. He wasn't sure he could go through the discomfort of the last few days again. Then he realized he would, if that was what it took to keep Bethany as a friend.

He smiled to himself at the thought of her romantic name, so totally at odds with her independent persona. So unusual, and so suitable to the woman he sensed underneath the thick shell. This morning she had slipped away early, obviously thinking she would leave before he could rise to confront her.

After a night no less restless than the last three had been, he'd been waiting for her to leave since dawn. He'd been ready to interfere if she turned to go around the house, uphill to where the vehicles were parked. But she and the mahogany buffoon struck out for the woods. Her hair had once more been hidden away, by both cap and scarf. No doubt extra pins had been added as well, to control any remote indication of softness.

He felt his smile increasing, at both the idea she could believe herself unfeminine and at the photo in his hands. Bethany and Baron had been trapped by the camera in a moment of extremely silly seriousness, fighting over the rights to one of her shoes. Such heavy coverings for such delicate feet. He wondered how much more tired those shoes made her by the end of the day. When would she allow him to massage away the aches?

Jonathan lifted his head, suddenly aware of the silence of the house around him. Never one to deny himself his indulgences, he worked with a constant soundtrack of his favorite songs, both classical and modern. The background sounds were there, but there was also an underlying hush, as though something had happened to destroy the peace of the forest.

He passed his forearm across his brow. Pushing back his hair and pushing away the idea, he finished the set of photos he'd been working on. The rest were at a point he could leave for a while. He glanced at his watch, suddenly very aware of the passage of time since Bethany and Baron had gone into the woods that morning.

Stepping out of the room, he reached the stereo unit in three impatient strides. Usually wild birds gathered outside, squabbling over seeds and occasionally accompanying the man-made music with natural harmony. There were birds glutting themselves at the feeders, some more attached to the suet ball. But none were singing.

He moved through the glass door onto the deck. The house had been planned to command a panoramic view of the valley below, with a deck added to extend that view. Search as he might, he could see no sign of Bethany. And it had become very important that he see her immediately.

With no way of knowing how far she had traveled in the hours she'd been gone, he couldn't begin to judge where she might be. For the first time in his life, he cursed the single mindedness of his personality, the character trait that made it possible for him to focus on the job at hand, shutting out any distractions.

In the past this made it possible for him to create images of unsurpassed beauty, unaware until the shoot was over that he was hip deep in frozen water or perched precariously on the limb of a swaying tree. This morning he'd lost track of time and hadn't been aware until just now that Bethany had been gone far too long for even the most exhausting of contemplative walks.

A sound came to him, drifting up on the cooling breeze. After a moment it was repeated, the nearly hoarse bark of a dog that had almost given up sending out its signal. Putting his fingers to his mouth, Jonathan whistled as he hadn't since he was a young boy, playing Indian scout in the woods with his brother.

The bark sharpened, repeating itself in an idiot-like frenzy. From the direction, he knew Baron was in a remote part of the forest. Moving purposefully, Jonathan charged back into the house to grab what he needed.

CHAPTER 6

I f you were really worth anything, you'd go for help. Lassie would have had the Marines here by now," Bethany said sternly to the dog below her. Then again, she reminded herself, Lassie could have called for a stand-in. All Baron could do was look up at her with his head tilted, foolish tongue hanging out the side of his mouth. As first he had barked ferociously, frustrated because he couldn't get up in the tree with her, angry because she wouldn't come down and play with him. "It is, after all, your fault."

In all honesty, she had to admit it was as much her fault as Baron's. True, she'd slipped when the setter, fast on the heels of a slow rabbit, had tumbled into a ditch, yelping piteously as he lost his footing. But it had been her own idiotic impulse, born of a long denied desire, that encouraged her to climb the tree in the first place. Branches set close together and a convenient vine had aided and abetted in her juvenile whim. The same branches and vine served to trap her foot and score her hands deeply when she attempted to scramble out of the tree with more enthusiasm than thought.

They wouldn't have wandered to an unknown section of the woods if her mind had been on where she was going rather than what had happened the night before. She'd left early that morning, too embarrassed to face Jonathan. The walk and her thoughts, after a night of too much thinking and not enough sleep, had brought her nothing but the realization that she could not continue to stay in J. Phillip Merritt's house. Not and maintain control over her emotions and her life. If she started within the next few hours, she could be halfway to San Francisco before the evening.

Bethany had no worry Jonathan would try to stop her. She'd heard the curse he was too polite to voice out loud. No doubt he was disgusted by her reaction to his simple kindness. How much more offended would he have been if he realized her normally subdued emotions had been threatening to riot? It had been thoroughly ingrained in her that men wanted to do their own chasing. A man like

Jonathan would have been appalled if she suddenly threw herself into his arms.

She'd known men like him in the past, men who were sophisticated and in full control of themselves. Men who expected the same level of poise and gracious composure in their women. That kind of man had no patience with nervous, flighty women who panicked at the most casual contact. She'd learned long ago that she could never be that cosmopolitan kind of woman, no matter how much she might want to try.

It was a shame she couldn't face him on an equal footing and take her leave maturely. Instead, she would have to wait until he came after her, found her, and helped her out of the tree. That he would come looking for her she had no doubt. No matter how unwelcome his houseguest had become, Jonathan would never abandon her. She only hoped he would get there before too much longer. It wasn't exactly warm in the deep forest.

かかか

At first, Jonathan wasn't sure he'd come to the right place, in spite of the dog dancing at his feet, and he worried about finding her in time. Night came early this deep in the woods, and travel was necessarily slow among the granite outcroppings and fallen trees. If Bethany were seriously hurt, it would be a major undertaking to get her back up the hill after he found her.

Baron dashed up to him again, actually taking hold of his sleeve and pulling as though he had a thought in his head he needed to convey. For lack of better direction, Jonathan gave in to the urging. Once he took a step forward, the quivering red dog dashed away again to take up his post at the foot of a thickly leaved tree, looking up and whining.

She'd somehow managed to wedge herself in a fork of the tree. Her arms embraced the trunk, further support being added by the over-shirt she'd wrapped around her body, tying the sleeves to a sturdy branch. A quick inspection showed him the problem, branches and a vine holding her foot at an angle too awkward for her to free herself. From the scarring on her heavy leather shoe, it was obvious she'd tried. Of course she would try. Bethany had taken care of herself too long to wait around for anyone to help.

Her face was pale against the leaves, a few stray freckles standing out starkly. Thick auburn lashes lay on the dark purple smudges defining the tops of her cheekbones. She seemed to be resting, or passed out, her mouth tightened as though to keep in any sound of distress.

"Bethany?" Something, perhaps the speed of his search, had caused a slight constriction in his throat. Clearing it, he tried again. "Bethany? Honey, how bad is it?"

The lashes quivered, compressing briefly then parting to reveal soft, mossy-colored eyes. In the twilight world of the not quite awake, she blinked then focused on him. Her mouth quivered, stretched into a small smile.

"Hello," she said, barely above a whisper. "I knew you'd come." She attempted to straighten herself, and the unwary move reminded her of why she was still in the tree. "I seem to be sort of stuck."

"Don't move. Let me take care of it." Let me take care of you, his mind added, but he knew better than to say it.

He worked quickly, efficiently, to pry the vines and branches apart with his hiking stick until he could gently remove her foot. Even then, she was held in the tree by her over-shirt and couldn't seem to pick the knot apart. Once he'd climbed up next to her, he understood why her hands didn't work as well as they could. None of the abrasions on her palms were deep, but there was enough surface damage to cause considerable pain and swelling.

He was able to loosen the knot, releasing her without cutting the shirt. She was going to need all the warmth he could give her. Wrapping her hands in the shirt and his handkerchief, he eased her out of the tree. All the while, he heard her soft words: "I knew you would come."

There was a stream not far from the tree, merrily dancing its way off the snow pack to eventually spill into Eagle Lake. With Bethany trying to help, he was able to maneuver her to a low point in the bank. Every emotion screamed at him to get her to the house *now*, but Jonathan knew if he didn't take the time to look at her foot and field dress her hands, the trip would take even longer. If they made it at all that night. They had to make it.

Using the backpack as a cushion, he braced her against a granite outcropping, folded back her jeans and reached for her shoe. Before she could protest he had his knife out and the laces slit. There was no time for finesse. It was lucky he didn't have to cut off the shoe itself.

He inspected her foot thoroughly, probing gently along all the joints, trying not to notice how delicate it was. Her elegant high arch was quickly becoming obliterated by the rapid swelling. Sliding his arm around her, murmuring an apology in her ear, he thrust the foot into the icy rushing water. His hand went under with the foot.

Cold. So incredibly, terribly cold. He had known it would be. Bethany struggled but the cold would help her, swiftly numbing her foot and taking the swelling down. He murmured soft words, and for the moment, it seemed she almost forgot not to trust, turning instinctively toward what warmth she could find.

Jonathan cursed himself and held her as closely as he dared while still forcing her foot into the water. He didn't know how long she'd been in the tree, but the swelling had to be reduced before he could wrap her foot and get her back to his house. No matter how much she fought, no matter how deeply her whimpers of protest scored his soul, he had to do this. Then she turned in his arms, breathing his name and snuggling against him.

For a moment he froze, almost afraid to react. He'd given in to his urges the night before and forced her into the woods to be injured. She was simply seeking comfort and warmth. Certainly he could control his animal impulses long enough to provide that.

Unfastening his jacket he pulled her closer, drawing the special thermal blanket out of the back pack and tucking it around her. His chin brushed against the solid knot of her hair. With no further compunction he removed the cap, scarf and the excess myriad of pins. She relaxed so suddenly he was afraid she'd fainted, but her color was good, her breathing even and deep.

There was a thermos of hot coffee in the backpack, along with bandages, aspirin and other necessities. He needed to tend her injuries so they could get under way. But for now, for this moment, he held her against his heart, feeling the soft crush of her breasts against his chest, her breath warm against his neck, and felt something deep inside him start to crack open.

Jonathan never again wanted to experience anything like that climb up the hill. They were in a location impossible to bring in any wheeled vehicle, too awkward in places to use any kind of stretcher arrangement. He found himself, for once, envying muscle worshipers who devoted hours every day to building up their bodies. Bethany helped where she could, leaning on his walking stick as well as his shoulder. But her ankle was up to only very light weight and no sudden movements, and he knew he could carry her only for short distances.

Long before they broke into the clearing, he cursed the impulse that had driven him to build near the top of a mountain. Pompous ass that he'd been, he wanted to be above it all, away from the filth he'd experienced, not realizing at the time that the filth had become a part of him. Now he would have cheerfully dynamited the whole damned mountain to make the journey one step shorter.

Once they were clear of the trees and on more level ground where he didn't have to worry about his own footing, he bent to lift her in his arms.

"Jonathan, no, it's not that much further. I can make it."

"Hush now. Let me demonstrate my macho masculine impulses. A real man would have been able to carry you all the way."

His self-derisive humor brought a tiny smile to her tautly held mouth. She looped her arms around his neck. Her head fell naturally against his shoulder, and she closed her eyes against the pain, as if finally trusting him to keep her safe.

$\wp \wp \wp$

Her own muffled whimper brought Bethany awake with a start. She stared across the room, tense and at first disoriented. Her face was turned to the banked fire, where glowing coals offered warmth and a promise of comfort. She thought about raising her head but was stopped by a feeling of intense lassitude.

She stirred, restless, not ready to go back to the sleep she knew she needed. Stronger twinges of soreness ran through her overall body aches, particularly her ankle and hands.

Still, the swelling seemed to have gone down and there didn't seem to be anything seriously wrong. At least, not physically.

Easing onto her back she sighed, and glared up at the high dark ceiling. She was in the living room. Jonathan had gone to the trouble of bedding her down on the soft leather couch to save her the inconvenience of the open steps between the bathroom and her bedroom.

She felt a great sadness welling up through the physical discomfort. Jonathan was the kind of person she'd wanted to meet when she was still worth knowing. It was too late now, and this most recent stupidity of hers would make it even more difficult for her to leave gracefully. She only hoped she could do it before she left too much of herself behind.

She shifted back onto her side, absently rubbing Baron's ears with the back of her hand when he stuck his head up for some attention. A soothing ointment had been rubbed on her palms, and her hands were loosely wrapped in gauze. Soft flannel encased her arms, and she remembered the clothing that had been thrust into her hands before she was sent into the warmed bathroom to wash off. The dark blue gown, a gift from Neil's family, covered her completely, though the flow of loose material all over her body was unsettling.

A soft sound, a breath different from her own, brought her senses to screaming alert, and she turned her head on the pillow more quickly than was wise. The resultant flash of pain stopped her briefly, her eyes squeezing shut until the pain resumed a bearable-ache status.

Nestled in a swath of quilts and pillows similar to the one that covered and supported her, Jonathan slept in the deep leather arm-chair near the head of the couch. His head tilted at an awkward angle and his clever fingers were clasped across his stomach. A nerve twitched in his cheek, where a beard had begun to shadow his aristocratic and altogether too appealing high cheekbones and flat cheeks. Since he was fast asleep, obvious-ly worn out from helping her, she allowed herself the indulgence of looking at him.

It was a very temporary indulgence, her eyes were becoming increasingly heavy. Now that she knew he was close by, his mocca-sined feet propped on the same hassock that had supported her back the night before, the pressures eased. Gently, completely, the soft fog of exhaustion reclaimed her.

∾∾

Through barely slitted eyes, Jonathan watched Bethany drift in and out of sleep. Although his body should have been screaming out for rest, he felt only a pleasant sort of fatigue and found it no strain to doze in the chair instead of seeking his bed. It was as though he drew strength from the subtle beauty of the woman lying on his couch. As long as his presence didn't disturb her, he would indulge himself.

When she began to mumble, moving her head restlessly on the pillow until her hair was a tumble of dark silken fire, he tensed, waiting to go to her aid. Then she awoke with a start, her apprehension a palpable force in the room. As he had seen her do so many times, she brought herself under control, efficiently identifying her location and assessing her condition.

The flannel nightgown obviously confused her. He'd been surprised to find it in the back of a drawer, no doubt part of the extra clothing packed by Neil's wife. If she hadn't been worn down by everything that had happened that day, she would no doubt have put up more of an argument about wearing it. As it was, she'd limped out of the bathroom, leaning heavily on his stick with her hair pinned loosely on her head and the long skirt of his dark green robe swirling around her impossibly charming bare feet. That was when he knew he was in serious trouble.

He'd talked her out of the robe, thinking only of her comfort while she rested. The memory of how the soft flannel cupped her buttocks when she sank onto the couch caused him to shift abruptly, commanding his body to stand down. Hers was a wounded spirit, and he only made life more difficult for her. He'd indulged himself already by removing her hairpins, arranging her hair as a further pillow for her pale cheek.

She turned her head now, seeing him for the first time. Under the quilts, the tension visibly left her slender body. Within seconds she was deeply, bonelessly asleep. Jonathan let out the breath he hadn't known he was holding. On some deep level, Bethany trusted him. It was a rare and precious gift he hugged to himself as he fell asleep.

෴

Bethany came fully awake to the chill of an eager Irish setter nose. An arm slid behind her back, supporting her while a long-fingered hand wrapped around Baron's eager muzzle, pushing him firmly away.

"How are you feeling this morning?" Jonathan's voice was as mellow and rich as the scent of the freshly brewed coffee that teased her wake-up nerves.

The support was welcome, as the pain of the day before had developed into extreme weakness. She was equally grateful when the arm was removed as soon as the pillows were rearranged to support her back. There was too much more than mere comfort emanating from the strength of the hand that had stroked across her back while arranging her comfortably.

A coffee mug, only partially filled, was placed gently in her wrapped hands. She waited to answer him until she had taken the first sip, allowing the rich dark liquid to perform its magic.

"Much better now." Her eyes opened slowly as the coffee trickled down her throat. She stretched slightly, testing the strength and maneuverability of her aching body. "At least, some of me is."

"Hold still a minute. Let me...." Not waiting for her approval, he eased the tangle of quilts and sheets from around her leg, pulling the hassock up beside the couch to sit on it and slide her foot onto his leg.

His thigh muscles shifted under the arch of her foot. Bethany tensed at the unaccustomed intimacy of the contact but couldn't summon the strength to draw back her foot. After a moment she relaxed and even began to enjoy the subtle massage of his adroit fingers removing the wrap, probing delicately for sore areas.

"You do that well," she said somewhat breathlessly. "Are you a masseur in your off season?" What was meant to be a sophisticated, off-hand comment came out unexpectedly husky, with a catch at the end when one finger probed more deeply.

"Sorry." The fingers soothed now, moving down to squeeze along the arch of her foot, bringing unprecedented comfort and something more. "Actually, I think I may have had a foot fetish in a former life."

"It's all right now." Pushing herself upright, she sought to reclaim her foot from the electric heat of his touch that was far more alarming than any pain. She was disappointed when he relinquished the foot, allowing her to hide again beneath the quilts.

Impersonal hands rearranged the covers, smoothing out what had become a jumble of sheet and quilts before he took the now empty mug out of her hand. The gaze he bent upon her seemed only polite but there was a hidden depth in the blue glitter she didn't remember seeing before. His hand strayed to her head, idly smoothing back the tangle her hair had become. She steeled herself not to pull away and was shocked at the pleasure a gentle, undemanding touch could bring.

"It looks like you have only a light sprain," he said, tucking some hair behind her ear. "If I thought you'd stay put I'd bring in a tray. I suppose I should feel fortunate you stayed still this long." His voice was as gently impersonal as the fingers now combing through her hair. "If I let you get up for breakfast will you promise to take it easy and stay off your feet as much as possible today?"

Bethany wondered at the phrasing, at the soft, almost whimsical note in his voice. It wasn't the voice of the man who had so arrogantly arranged for her to come here. Nor was the gentle hand remotely connected to the image she was laboring to maintain of J. Phillip Merritt. Too many memories overlapped and she wondered how much was truly Jonathan, how much was eclipsed by her experiences.

"Food sounds good," she said cautiously. Her stomach agreed with an ill-mannered grumble and she found herself starting to smile even as she felt the heat rising in her face. "But I think I might kill for a shower."

"Do you really think you're up to a shower?"

"I really think I can't stand to be near myself much longer if I don't get one. I wonder how you've managed to tolerate me this long."

He wondered how fast she would run if he told her how sexy old sweat smelled on her.

Then he decided he would save that morsel for later.

"Do you have another gown you can change into? I really rather you didn't dress."

This time she did pull away, slamming up barricades so fast he could almost hear them clang.

"Take it easy." His words tumbled out on a storm of anger. "I save seductions for women in top physical condition. They're the only ones who can keep up with me. You're safe. For now."

Summoning a wry smile, she reached for the dark green robe conveniently draped across the back of the couch.

"Thanks for the reassurance," she said, as if attempting to regain the glib tone he'd become accustomed to hearing. "It almost encourages me not to rush my recovery." She struggled with the long robe, attempting to maintain both the covers and her dignity. It was a hopeless battle.

Jonathan was already cursing himself for the thoughtless comments. Now he found an unexpected corner of what he was beginning to recognize as his heart warming at her attempted insouciance. Keeping his touch as

145

impersonal as possible, he eased the robe across her back, pretending he didn't see the soft sway of her breasts against the front of her gown when she gave up the quilts to scramble her arms into the sleeves.

"Could you humor me in this, Bethany? I get the feeling if you were dressed you'd forget you'd been hurt and go racing outside if Baron barked at a squirrel."

Tossing back the quilts to the end of the couch, he slid an arm along her back as she rose and pulled the robe securely around herself. It was fortunate his arm was there when she swayed, biting back a cry as her foot came into contact with the floor. His immediate impulse, to sweep her into his arms and to the inviting expanse of his own bed, was squashed immediately.

"Let's compromise," he suggested. "One of the showers has a detachable head. I'll put a stool in there so you can sit down to wash if you agree to stay off your feet the rest of the day."

She frowned slightly, as if considering what she was hearing of the offer and what he wasn't asking. He knew he could have coerced her into complying by simply refusing to help her move around. Sighing, she gave in, subtly leaning against his strength.

"Marsha packed more gowns. No reason to let them go to waste, is there?"

⋐⋑⋐⋑

Later, washed, changed, and feeling marginally more human, Bethany sat trying to read a magazine, and wondered how people could stand to not be doing something every minute of the day. Jonathan had let her come into the kitchen for breakfast, but insisted she return to the couch after that. Tossing the magazine to one side, she blew out her breath in disgust.

"That certainly sounded melancholy," Jonathan said as he maneuvered a large tray through the doorway. "Don't you dare get up," he warned, when she moved to help him. "If you absolutely have to do something, push that coffee table over so I can put this down."

Once the tray was settled, and the ottoman moved so Jonathan could use it for a seat, he busied himself with the stereo system. Stirring Gaelic ballads filled the air. The music was emotionally intense and he turned the volume low, providing atmosphere rather than interference.

While he adjusted the music, Bethany examined the tray. Instead of the excellent coffee he normally brought, there was a smaller, delicate china pot, steaming with strongly brewed Earl Grey tea. A larger pot contained only hot water. She automatically set out small plates and napkins in front of their seats.

The music served as a background to the timeless ritual of afternoon tea, served in antique cups and accompanied by delicate pastries and small sandwiches. Very few words passed between them as Bethany poured, first strong tea then hot water, adding lemon and sugar as he indicated. The treats were transferred to his plate first, then hers. There was a comforting aspect to doing something, however small, for this man who'd done so much for her. The ritual was effortless for her, learned so long ago it seemed to be ingrained in her genes. Only when both of them were served did she take a delicate sip of her own tea. It was an excellent blend, perfectly brewed.

"What a wonderful idea." She closed her eyes to more completely sense the tea filling her with delicate strength. "Don't tell me you made all these lovely little pastries."

"Would you believe me if I said yes?" His voice was gently mischievous, and he chuckled when she merely looked at him, one brow raised. "Mail order and freezers, my dear." He held out his cup for more tea, watching her intensely as she once more performed the simple ritual.

"You do that as to the manor born," he observed, as she passed the cup back to him. "Perfectly prepared. My sisters would envy you."

Cup halfway to her mouth, she paused, frowning slightly. "I'm afraid you lost me."

"They either drop something, forget who takes sugar, or over fill the cup. No matter how hard they try, they never get that naturally elegant effect when serving tea. Peggy blames it on the American school system not teaching the finer aspects of entertaining."

She jerked suddenly, setting the cup down too quickly. Tea splashed over the edge, marking the linen napkin and running onto the table.

"Sorry," she said, a controlled quaver in her voice. "Guess you spoke too soon." At least her hands weren't trembling. That was a good thing. Not looking at him, she attempted to blot up the tea.

"Don't worry about it. Everything washes." When she wouldn't stop, he covered her hands with his. His long fingers were cool against her skin. Gently, he removed the soiled napkin from her grasp and tossed it to one side. "Relax, Bethany."

He released her hand before the trembling could start, this time as a foolish reaction to his touch. When he didn't speak, she finally raised her head to meet his concerned gaze. Holding eye contact, he sipped his tea then set down the cup, so elegantly it didn't seem at all incongruous that he was dressed in jeans and a mercifully fastened wool shirt. As if he had also perfected the technique in a far different setting.

Clearing her throat, Bethany dared to try her voice.

"Why would your sisters want to serve high tea?"

"They were fascinated by those old English movies where everyone wore fancy dresses and drank mass quantities of tea." He smiled as though at an old memory. "I don't know how many tea parties I attended, along with their dolls and whatever teddy bear was in favor that week." That surprised a giggle out of her, and he went on, seeming to choose his words carefully.

"Where did you learn to serve high tea?"

Not why, she realized, but where—as if possessing a useless anachronistic skill was perfectly normal. She decided to go along with his assumption.

"At school," she admitted, maintaining the calm she'd learned long before. "Unlike your sisters, I had the privilege of a European education."

He nodded, as if this were not a surprise, and disposed of a pastry in one inelegant bite. "Were your parents European?"

"Actually, they were Americans, who preferred to live in Europe." There was no need for him to know her mother's family had supported this preference, to keep them out of the public eye. "Since they travelled, I attended a boarding school and stayed with them during the breaks." She busied herself with more tea, grateful for the silly task. Might as well get all of it out in the open. After all, he was offering more of his past to her every day.

"After Mother died, it was more convenient for me to stay in the school year round. Sometimes I would visit the family of one of the other girls in the summer."

"What about your father?" he asked, as though only mildly interested, but there was an intense glitter in his eyes.

"I'm afraid my father wasn't really cut out to be a single parent." Nor could he have afforded to keep her in the summer. A trust fund, set up by her mother's will, had paid for her schooling. Again, nothing Jonathan needed to know about. She cast around for something that would remove the displeasure from his face. "Daddy did make it possible for me to go to a much better school, when I was a little older. That was where I learned such invaluable job skills as arranging flowers and serving high tea."

Anger and pity warred on his face. She could almost see the words trembling on his lips. In the end, he merely passed his plate for more delicacies, which she served in silence.

"We might as well take advantage of that schooling, so your skills don't get rusty.

While you are resting," he emphasized, with an attempt at a stern glare, "I have to get some things done in the darkroom."

It was all said very gently, but there was a new look to him. Not only the pity, but also something else, as though he thought he almost recognized her. Of course, this wasn't possible, for which she could thank the fates that had not always been so kind to her.

CHAPTER 7

I've been wondering about this one." Jonathan's voice was rich with expectant humor as he came around the end of the couch, sitting on the hassock and holding out a photograph from the collection in his hand. "Some of the others made sense, but this was beyond me."

"This" was a photograph that was more blur than image. In one corner, a suggestion of dark red hinted that Baron might have been in the general area. Tilting her head to one side, Bethany regarded the photo through squinted eyes. She could feel a frown developing between her brows. Then the frown cleared.

"I remember! It was windy, and Baron was chasing a leaf." She also remembered centering Jonathan in the viewfinder, and the image blurring when she realized how devastating he was to her senses. Her jolt of recognition had come as the shutter clicked. "I can't believe you printed these. Usually the lab just develops the negatives and asks me if I really want to have any of them printed."

"You did mention once that you wanted to be a wildlife photographer," he reminded her with a small smile. "I wondered if you had come up with some new technique."

"No, just the same old disasters." She sighed, shuffling through the out of focus, un-centered photos. They were so bad, she couldn't resent his subtle teasing. "Your camera is far more sensitive than any I've ever used before but that's really no excuse. When it comes to taking pictures, I guess I'm better—"

Her words were cut off abruptly as Jona-than removed the offending photos from her lap, replacing them with a different stack.

"What's this? Oh, my." Her voice trailed off as she studied an image of Baron stalking an offensive sock. The rest of the series showed him pouncing on the sock and putting it to a merciful death. "You took these, didn't you. When?"

The couch dipped beneath his weight as Jonathan rested one knee next to her hip. His hand, holding the offending photos, braced against the back of the couch. He reached to search among the prints in her lap. This brought his chest, hard and warm beneath the soft cotton sweater, close against her shoulder.

Bethany recognized the move for what it was, casual contact with an acquaintance. She would not allow herself to attach any undue importance to the warmth of him against her back, in spite of the fact that she felt something far different than she had ever felt before. Her breath caught and held, trapped somewhere between her chest and her throat. When he leaned even closer, when his breath softly stirred the loose hairs on her brow, her heart, that once dependable organ, began to swell, migrating up into her throat.

"Here it is. We were east of the house, looking at this stand of pine. We thought there might be a nest up there." The photo he found was amazing for its depth of detail. No birds were in sight, but a squirrel had stopped along its mad race on a branch to briefly consider the humans.

"I've never been able to get a shot like this. It's as though you had them trained." She took the photo from his hand to study it more closely, managing to avoid touching him in the process. She was afraid if she felt that spark that always seemed to jump between them when they touched, she would make more of a fool of herself than ever before. A caring Jonathan was even more devastating than one who was just being polite.

"I gave that up, remember?" His voice was harsher than ever before. Abruptly pushing away, he crossed the room and looked out the wide window into the late afternoon washed in gold by the setting sun.

She remembered what he'd once told her, about almost taming some of the wildlife and inadvertently causing deaths during a harsh winter. She cursed at herself for being so insensitive.

"Jonathan? I'm sorry. I—that was incredibly crass of me."

❧❧❧

He looked back at her from the window. The day's rest had taken some of the drawn look from her face though she still showed signs of strain around her deep forest eyes, and that lovely soft mouth still pinched in at the edges. Since her shower, she exuded her own personal scent, enticing him from across the room. He'd gone into the darkroom after tea to put distance between them while warring with himself.

She was made up of equal parts of innocence, vulnerability and a devastating sexiness that was entirely inadvertent and therefore even more deadly. He was being tortured over a fire of intense desire, wanting to enfold her and join with her irrevocably, while she avoided contact even with his fingers. Surely the gods were laughing.

He'd gotten too close there on the couch. Reaching over her shoulder, he'd very nearly thrown himself on her body. Not the best way to earn someone's trust.

Now she was blinking at him slowly. Apprehension showed in the depths of her eyes and in the way she first touched each corner of her mouth quickly, nervously, with her tongue before drawing one lower edge in between her teeth. He reminded himself again she didn't do it intentionally.

Sighing, he pushed away from the window, strolling back to her with a semblance of his normal insouciant grace and dropped onto the ever trustworthy hassock. He was within reaching distance of the photographs but in a safety zone relative to her body. He hoped.

Sorting through the stack of photos still in his hand, he held out one that was at least in focus, although it held no discernible subject matter.

"This one shows some promise."

"What would you consider naming it? 'Dull Day at Black Rock'? How about: 'Emptiness of a Writer's Mind'? I'm sorry," she said softly, daring to touch his arm. He saw her hand approaching, and was able to brace himself against the contact. "Actually, I may have been prompted by jealousy. I've never taken a picture one tenth as beautiful as your most casual pieces."

"We each have our own special talents. I've never described anything the way you wrote about my book."

"So you did like it after all. I wondered, the way you came across in Neil's office." Her voice teased subtly, with a catch of nervous laughter, and the cloud of tension began to dissipate.

"When I decided to come into the city and meet the person who knew more about my soul than even I did, I didn't expect someone like you. If I forgot to say so before, once I got past the shock, I did like the piece, very much."

"You should have seen the one I didn't submit." She had become so relaxed the reply came out without conscious thought.

"You've said something like that before," he pointed out, a note of amusement running through his voice. "When are you going to let me see this infamous piece?"

This time when her lower lip slipped between white teeth it was to control a small impish smile that etched a crease in one cheek. "I don't think you're ready for that just yet."

To forestall any further discussion, she turned back to the pictures in her hands, idly sorting through them.

"Will any of these be used in a book?"

"It's hard to say. I'm not really sure what the next book will be about." He was not about to tell her his growing hope that these photos, and the ones she hadn't seen yet, would be part of a family picture album. "Have you ever considered writing a book yourself?"

She seemed to give the question her fullest attention, though it was hard to read much in her downturned face. After a few moments of shuffling through the photos she shrugged, looking up at him from the corner of her eye.

"I think everyone with access to paper and pen has considered writing a book at one time or another. But I'm not enough of an authority on anything to write non-fiction, and it's always seemed to me that you have to have experienced life to write about it."

"You've led an exciting enough life."

Bethany gathered up the photos and placed them on the table next to the couch. "What makes you say that?"

Jonathan was shocked at the sudden change in her. The pinched look came back in her face, which was at least three shades lighter than it had been. What had he said?

"You've created a unique life style for yourself, going anywhere your fancy draws you, meeting unusual people, getting them to share their lives with you. That kind of freedom would be the envy of many people."

"Every freedom has its price. I can pick up and go wherever the next subject is, but Paul's is as close as I get to having a home, and he's just a stopover."

Now it was his turn to concentrate on the photos in his hand. He wasn't familiar with the sudden rush of emotion he felt, but he very much feared it might be jealousy. Whatever the driving force behind his desire to yell, rant, and rave, he knew he had to choose his next words very carefully.

"How did you meet Paul, anyway?" He applauded his casual tone.

"Baron was sick once, shortly after I got him. I didn't realize there was any difference in dog foods. When I ran out of the food his breeder had given me, I just grabbed whatever was convenient."

"I take it not all foods agree with Irish stomachs."

"Mmmm. I was on the road when he started going down. By the time I could find a vet opened, he was barely holding on. It took almost a week to get the mutt back on his feet." She reached out a stockinged foot to run it along the ecstatic dog's back.

So the Nordic god was a hero and lifesaver, too. Wonderful. He probably ran a child support clinic on the side.

"What a good way to meet a friend."

"I didn't think so at the time. For the first two hours, while he was doing everything he possibly could to give Baron a chance to fight for his life, all Paul did was bitch about how poorly I cared for my dog. I finally convinced him it was ignorance rather than neglect that had caused the problem."

"Did he back down then?"

"Paul believes ignorance is no excuse. When I told him I'd never had a dog before, he decided to reserve judgment until he saw how well I cared for Baron once the ignorance problem was solved."

"Now that you're best friends, is Paul's your permanent base?"

"It's a convenient stopover for now. I can wash the kid off there on my way in. When I have extra time, I grab a real shower for myself. Usually, I just take care of Baron on the run, and use the shower in Neil's office. It's much better than the one in my rig."

"You've built a hell of a life for yourself, BL Acton."

"Is that meant as a compliment or a complaint, Mr. Merritt?" she asked gently, with none of the usual underlying tension in her voice.

"Just another observation." Along with the complex, independent lifestyle she'd built for herself, she'd also built a maze of walls around her emotions. Even now, when she was more relaxed than she'd probably been in years, she kept her inner self separate from him. At best, the walls had been reduced to fences. High fences.

Shaking his head, he rose to his feet, striding out of the room. He returned as abruptly as he had left, reaching down to remove the photos in her lap before extending a hand to her in invitation.

"Enough of this lazing about, woman. If I can't hold your interest with little pictures, I'll try big ones."

∾∾∾

She regarded the proffered hand seriously. It was a nice hand, well-shaped and strong. It had proven to be a skilled hand, dispensing comfort and care in generous doses. Now it was a very tempting hand. In a moment of great daring, she gave in to temptation.

Raising her chin until their gazes locked, she slowly accepted the invitation of the hand, taking it between both of hers and clasping firmly. His long fingers curled around her wrist in a warm grasp that was somehow far more than comforting. With a gentle tug, he pulled her to her feet, bracing her until the walking stick could be slipped into her palm. Only then did he step away, and somehow the room got suddenly cooler.

"Come see my etchings, my dear."

His voice was so melodramatically deep, so comically sinister, Bethany followed without protest. This day, this time together, had been outside of any former experience for her. She knew it could not last. One day, Jonathan would lose interest in her apparent lack of sophistication and the bizarre life she now led.

Or, one day, Jonathan would somehow learn the truth about her life. On that day, any kindly thoughts he might have about her would be gone forever. Until then, she would take every precious golden minute she could steal and hoard them against a bleak future. Firm in this resolve, she followed his carefully paced steps across the living room and down the hall to what she knew was his studio, though she hadn't been invited there before.

As they stepped into a room bathed in the fading flames of an autumn sunset, Jonathan relinquished his supporting hold. He was hurrying forward to shift a stool, creating a clear path, and didn't see her sag against the door frame, her gaze fixed on the opposite wall. But he apparently heard the gasp of a quickly indrawn breath.

"Bethany? Honey, are you all right?" He was back by her side instantly, daring to slide an arm around her. "You're shivering. I knew I shouldn't have let you get up today."

Without asking further permission he bent, lifting her in his arms for the few steps into the room. She held herself rigid, fighting the subtle chills racking her body. He set her gently on an overstuffed chair, lifting her feet onto a stool and covering her immediately with a quilt.

"Can I get you anything? Soup, coffee, brandy?" Still she didn't respond, only sat with her lower lip clenched tightly between her small teeth, eyes squeezed shut.

"Dammit, Bethany, what's wrong?" His voice changed his voice from gentle concern to sharp query.

The all too familiar masculine demand cut through layers of cold shock and brought her abruptly back to the present. Drawing a deep breath, she marshaled her thoughts. It would require tremendous finesse, but she could get through this if she could maintain control.

"How very foolish of me." She spoke in the cultured tones drilled into her until they became automatic. "I must have stepped down wrong on my foot. Thank you so much for your gallant rescue."

ひのひ

Her lashes swept up, revealing eyes of indeterminate green. There were no forest glade secrets, no lost fairy princess images. Just opaque green eyes and a distant, polite voice. He frowned abruptly but, sensing questions about to be answered, refrained from comment.

"What a lovely yacht. Is it yours?"

The yacht was depicted in a poster-sized photograph, set against a sky of intense blue with water foaming at the bow. It was a portrait of excessive beauty, absolute freedom and extreme wealth. It was his reminder to himself of what he least enjoyed remembering.

"No, it wasn't. There's quite a story behind that beauty, though not a very nice one."

She indicated, with the lift of a thick brow and the wave of one elegantly curved hand, that the story would interest her. Her face seemed to convey total absorption in his words. Every gesture, every expression, was skillfully gracious, calculated to encourage him.

He strode away from her to stare out the window, wondering how little he could tell her and still satisfy her abrupt interest. There was something very wrong here, something to do with the evilly beautiful boat that symbolized so much that had been wrong in his world. But what did that have to do with her?

"It belonged to someone I knew of through mutual acquaintances. It's not the yacht itself that is interesting as much as how he acquired it." Jonathan kept his back to her, not sure if he wanted to continue with this.

"And how was that?"

"He sold his only daughter into marriage with a man more than twice her age to get that damned barge."

"What an utterly appalling tale." The words come out perfectly enunciated. "Were you acquainted with the individual who paid such a price for his bride?"

He felt as though he'd been dropped into the middle of a wicked farce. The gentle sprite he'd been cultivating had disappeared, along with her haunted alter egos. In their place was a carefully schooled socialite with less life than a department store mannequin.

Coming to a quick decision he moved toward a wall of cupboards, searching for memories, and answers. He found and pulled out an album. Briefly, he considered not digging any further, just letting the moment go by. Bethany had never looked more remote, or more fragile. But the same devil that had once controlled his every action was riding him now. He set the album in her lap, flipping open the leather bound cover.

"How fortunate I was still photographing people then. I have the entire cast immortalized on film." He strove to maintain a similar pseudo bored tone of voice. "Here's the yacht again, the day he took possession. Called her the 'Little Lulu,' in honor of his beloved daughter. The groom here, with a few hundred of his closest, most intimate friends, on the wedding day. Quite the aristocrat, wouldn't you say?" His cold, ruthless voice didn't allow her to respond. "And somewhere in here—ah, yes. The virgin sacrifice. Poor silly little bit of fluff."

The bride wore white. White veil, white shoes, white bikini cut high on legs made even longer by the four inch heels that had made walking dangerous and standing a torture. Short dark hair had been brushed forward in a gamine style emphasizing her eyes, made even larger and darker by the makeup, and drugs, they had used to turn her into a lovely, willing bride. And over it all the exquisite veil, handmade by nuns who were no doubt horrified when they heard the details of the marriage. The veil that was a symbol of why the wedding farce was taking place, proof to the world of what she was at that moment, what she would be for the next three years. Stefan DuBec's virgin bride.

CHAPTER 8

Come on, kid. It won't be so bad if you keep moving. We're almost there." Bethany wondered if the encouragement was for her dog or herself.

The ground was cold beneath her stockinged feet, when she could manage to keep her feet under her. It had also been cold beneath her knees and the barely healed palms of her hands. But there wasn't time to think about that now. There'd been no time to think about anything since she stepped into Jonathan's studio and saw the photo of her father's yacht on the wall.

Why Jonathan had that photo, and the portraits of her wedding, were questions she would have to explore later. After she had gotten away. She wanted to be far away from him before he started to put the pieces together and realized he'd been a witness to the depravity of her life.

He'd been unfailingly polite that evening, she thought as she rested briefly against the slender trunk of a young birch tree. She stroked Baron's upturned face, seeking to hush his worried whines. Giving up on story-telling, Jonathan had helped her back to the couch, fed her dinner, and kept her company until she could convince him she was too tired to keep her eyes open another second. She'd lain very still on the couch, drawing on years of experience to give every impression of a person deeply asleep.

It had obviously worked. After spending time between the kitchen and his studio, looking in on her every few minutes, Jonathan had finally gone into his room, closing the door gently. Soft music accompanied the shadows moving in the light under his door, continuing for a while after the light went out. Then the silence had been absolute.

When she was positive he would be asleep, she'd left, taking only the robe and her dog. Anything else could be replaced or sent to her, depending on his mood in the morning. The article, the interview that would have been such a coup, would be written by some-one else. No doubt Jonathan would agree this was the best possible way to part, especially if he ever figured out who she really was.

It was obvious from his words that evening that the self-proclaimed beautiful people disgusted him. Whether she'd been a willing participant or truly a victim was immaterial. She had been a part of the set, and for that there was no excuse.

Stifling a sob of what she was sure was relief, she fell against the driver's door. It was unlocked, as always when she was out of the city, and the keys would be in the ignition. She eased open the door, reaching immediately to turn off the interior light, and urged Baron to scramble past her while she rested gratefully against the seat.

In just a minute, she would get into the seat, turn the key and flip the levers that would blow heat off the engine. Getting into the motorhome would be difficult, but she had come too far now to give up. She straightened, bracing one hand on the seat, curling the other around the steering column, below the ignition and the dangling key ring.

The keys weren't there.

For a moment she groped along the steering column, unable to believe what her sore

173

fingers were telling her. There was no brass ring hanging there, big enough that she couldn't lose it. There was nothing.

The cold breeze wafting up under her gown was balmy when compared to the ice floes forming in her blood stream. She rarely took the keys out of the motorhome when she was on assignment. It was too easy to lose them. Once or twice she had dropped them under the driver's seat, although she didn't recall doing so this trip.

Muttering dire threats to the missing keys, she released the steering column, ducking under the wheel to check the floor beneath the seat. It was awkward but there was no other way to check, especially without a light.

Illumination was provided suddenly, when the passenger door was flung open, and the beam of a powerful flashlight was aimed directly into her face.

"Looking for something, Ms. Acton?"

Forgetting where she was, reacting only to the frigid, biting anger in his voice, Bethany straightened abruptly. The hastily pinned up thickness of her hair was all that saved her skull from a far too intimate acquaintance with the steering column. Dazed by the blow she'd given herself and the relentless glare, she fell against the driver's seat.

"My keys." Her voice was a weak imitation of itself. "Do you know where my keys are?"

"What happened, Ms. Acton? Did I get too close to the sanctity of your retreat? For a while there, you were almost acting like a real woman. Is that what sent you running again?" It was difficult to see his expression beyond the light, but the cold mockery in his voice left little doubt about his attitude. Bethany ignored his words, though the bitter tone chilled the ice that had taken her over. This could be endured, as she had endured everything else.

"If you please, Mr. Merritt. I would like the keys to my vehicle. Do you know where they are?" Every word was precisely enunciated.

His free hand appeared in the light, the errant key ring dangling from one long finger. Forgetting herself briefly, Bethany reached out, only to see the keys closed within his hand.

"No. First, you come back into the house and get a decent night's rest. When you're fit to travel, you'll get your keys, and not a moment before. In the meantime, you'll explain to me what prompted this latest foolishness."

"I will explain nothing to you, Mr. Merritt. You have no right to detain me."

"I'm holding your keys in my hand. That gives me all sorts of rights." The light never wavered, nor did the implacability of his tone. "We can stay out here and freeze for the rest of the night if you want, but I'm dressed for it far better than you are. I suggest you come back inside."

There had been a time in her life when Bethany had been conditioned to automatically obey a command so clearly issued. She had reconditioned herself. Gathering her dignity, she straightened regally.

"I don't think so, Mr. Merritt. If you insist on holding my keys ransom, I have no control over your actions. I can as easily stay out here as come into the house and, quite honestly, at the moment the atmosphere out here is far more to my liking."

She'd expected an explosion of some sort, either intense masculine anger or cynical laughter. What she got was a deep sigh and a sudden lowering of the light. The level of tension dropped dramatically.

"Enough, Bethany." The door across from her was eased shut, and she heard him walking slowly around the front of the motorhome. "We both know your heater's out. Come in for the rest of the night and you can leave when it's light, if you really think you have to."

She turned as he approached, wary at the abrupt change in his attitude. There was too much of a dichotomy to this man, and his kindness unsettled her even more than his anger. She busied herself with calling a very confused Irish setter out again and closing the door firmly once Baron was on the ground.

The flashlight illuminated only the ground between them, revealing his low boots and well-worn jeans. In the backwash she could see his leather coat open over a snug sweater. He had obviously taken time to dress once he realized she'd left. She kept herself as far back as possible from the glow, not needing a lecture on the inappropriateness of her own attire.

"Where are your shoes?" Having made this much of a discovery about her attire, he didn't hesitate to illuminate the rest of her, including the mud on her knees, the redness around her eyes and tense, pain induced lines imbedded near her mouth. "What in the world have you done to yourself? What could possibly have caused you to do anything this foolish?"

It was the wrong question, at the wrong time. She forgot caution, forgot her pride or any desire to salvage something of this association. Raising her chin, she drew in one last strengthening breath.

"What else would you expect from a 'poor, silly little bit of fluff'?" Her voice was suddenly, utterly calm.

"Bethany?" There was so much in that word, wrenched from a tightening throat. "What are you talking about?"

"Figure it out for yourself, smart man. Once you do, you won't want me around. In the interest of efficiency, just give me the keys now and let me go. I don't really think I'll be up to another trek up this hill any time soon." Her voice was still toneless but there was a slight break she couldn't control at the end of the sentence.

Jonathan held the key ring up, as if studying the way the moonlight glinted off the shapes and edges of metal. Then he closed his fingers around the keys and pushed them deep into the pocket of his leather jacket.

"I don't think so, honey," he said softly, moving closer to her and taking a gentle hold of her arm above the elbow. "Whatever you're trying to say, whatever you've been hiding from me, you can't go anywhere until you feel better. Hold this."

He pushed the flashlight into her slack hands. Bending abruptly, he slid one arm behind her knees, one around her waist, and lifted her high against his chest. She remained stiff, unyielding in his arms, but he apparently decided to ignore the cold stillness that radiated off her.

⁊ᴐᴇᴐ

Bethany felt encased in a cocoon of gentle warmth. Pillows behind her head and under her foot offered maximum comfort on the wide leather couch. Thick dry socks had replaced the damp ones, and the numbness in her toes was gradually receding. She'd given up the robe. At that point, it seemed senseless to argue about a robe when her whole life was in danger of being exposed to him.

Quilts were pulled up to her chin, and her hair had been taken down and spread across the pillows under her head. After building up the fire, Jonathan returned to sit, not on the hassock, but on the edge of the couch, facing her, his thigh resting snugly against her hip. Except for the alarming moments in her camper, it was the closest a man had been to her for seven years. Even through the layers of cloth and quilt, she felt his intense body heat.

"You're crowding me," she protested weakly, trying to edge into the back of the couch and away from his disturbing warmth.

"Tough. We've done it your way for almost a week now. I've avoided touching you until I ache to the back of my teeth, and still you pull this stunt." He braced one hand against the back of the couch, leaning over her, pinning her down with his presence if not his actual body. "Now we're going to do it my way. Talk to me, Bethany."

Staring into the cool clear blue of his eyes, she waited for the panic, knowing that this time she wouldn't be able to control it. But it never came. The days of undemanding companionship he was complaining about had changed her. She let his face, his eyes, fill her whole field of vision and still felt nothing but an intense curiosity. A muscle twitched at one corner of his mouth and he swallowed, causing a ripple to pass down his throat.

Her gaze followed that ripple until it descended into the V-neck of his dark blue sweater, then she looked back into his face. Her mouth felt suddenly dry at the increasing intensity of the blue in his eyes, and she slipped her tongue out quickly to wet her lips, pulling the lower lip back in to chew on. This seemed to fascinate Jonathan. His gaze dropped to her mouth and he leaned closer, almost too close, before his dark lashes lowered, and he straightened abruptly.

"Stop that." He looked away for a moment, into the fire. When he looked back again, meeting her eyes, he sighed. He lifted an unsteady hand, cupping her chin while his slightly calloused thumb stroked along her jaw, gently freeing the abused lip. "Unless you want me to forget all the promises I made to myself, you'll stop looking at me like that."

"Like what?" Was that really her voice, that soft murmur with a break at the end?

"Like you'd die happy if you could feel my breath joining with yours."

Now the panic came. Disregarding the pain shooting up her leg, she scrambled backwards up the pillow. If she couldn't get out any other way, she'd get away over the end of the couch.

She got no further than out from under the quilts before he caught her.

Reacting quickly, he grasped her waist, holding her down in spite of her struggles. Desperation lent her strength, but not enough. Gasping for air, she fell back against the pillows, shrinking from the feel of his weight against her body. Now it would come. Whatever had restrained him before this had ceased to have control. Now he would hold her down, dominate her, demonstrate his superiority over her.

∽∾∽∾

First he felt the cold rigidity return to her slender body. Then faint ripples moved through her like gasping breaths. Keeping his hands on her shoulders in gentle restraint, he levered his own body up, once more sitting beside her on the couch. Now, instead of stoically accepting his touch or shyly welcoming his warmth, her body rejected his existence totally. She was there physically, but the rest of her was hidden deeply away. Her reactions spoke of experiences so disturbing he did not want to guess at them.

He searched for words but couldn't think of any that would soothe her. How could he convince her that, whatever had happened in her past, he wouldn't hurt her? Withdrawing his hands from her shoulders, he reached for the disordered quilts, smoothing them until she was once again covered to her chin. He could not completely control the need to touch her. For now, he contented himself with holding the very ends of her silky hair between his fingers. Counseling himself to patience, he watched her.

ᴄᴈᴄᴈ

When the attack did not continue, when his body lifted away from hers and his weight no longer pinned her to the couch, Bethany was confused. When he re-arranged the coverings, offering her at least an illusion of modesty, she was shocked. But when he didn't continue even the verbal interrogation, she was totally consumed with curiosity.

At first, she subdued her unusual reaction. His continuing silence, though he did not move from her side, finally brought her eyes open.

He was waiting for her, a slight frown between eyes so filled with concern, at first she could only stare. Then his mouth quirked into a one-sided smile and he raised his hand to cautiously push the hair back from her face.

"Hello there," he said, his voice pitched intentionally low. "Back for a quick visit, or are you intending to stay for a while?" His hand rested against her cheek, offering warmth but demanding nothing in return.

She found the gentle whimsy dangerously enticing, and wondered what would happen if she allowed herself to fall under the spell of this aspect of Jonathan Merritt. Then she reminded herself severely she'd met too many sides to this man to be able to trust him.

"We need to talk about this, Bethany." He turned away as he spoke, once more staring into the fire. "What spooked you tonight? Everything seemed to be fine until you saw the picture of that damned yacht. What could you possibly have to do with Stefan Dubec and his..." Eyes widening, he turned on her. "What you said outside, about some 'poor silly little bit of fluff.' But her name was Lulu. I remember everyone talking about her at the wedding."

"Bethany Louise. No proper Frenchman could pronounce my first name. Besides, they thought 'Little Lulu' was cuter." Her voice sounded strained to her own ears. She wondered how long this would go on. Already she could see signs of his withdrawal. "I never wanted to have it all," she whispered. "I would have been happy with just a small portion."

She studied his face, softened in the flickering light, saving up a few more precious moments. His concern was unsettling. It was obvious he had not fully comprehended the situation. "I don't feel like talking about this right now, Jonathan." Her voice was tight, clipped. "You don't need to stand guard over me. I won't leave without telling you. You might as well get some more sleep. I'm planning to."

Taking a firm hold on the quilts, she shifted until she faced the back of the couch. She squeezed her eyes shut. Maybe if she could pretend hard enough that she was asleep, it would really happen.

When she felt the couch shift as he lifted his weight away from her, Bethany told herself she was relieved. Soon the truth would sink in, and he'd be only too happy to let her go. For tonight, for just now, she could pretend they were still friends, and maybe just a little more. When the moisture trickled across the bridge of her nose, she told herself it was perspiration, though the core of her body remained cold. It couldn't be a tear. Those had dried up long ago.

ભઝ

She was starting to stir. For two hours she'd faced the back of his couch, effectively shutting him out of her life and her thoughts. The quilt-covered curves had moved only enough to indicate light breathing. An occasional quickly drawn breath, not quite a sob, warned him she wasn't resting as well as he might want. He had dozed from time to time, once more ensconced in the armchair that could have been big enough for the two of them, but not for their memories. Not their pasts.

He should have remembered. Dubec's bride's eyes had been remarkable. Huge, bewildered, they dominated her face and overshadowed every one of the horde attending the travesty of a wedding. It had been Bethany's eyes, in Chandler's office, that first caught his attention.

What a difference. On the yacht she'd been lost, as though her last friend had betrayed her. She'd done exactly what she was told to do, and stood meekly when left alone. Often she'd seemed on the verge of tears.

Back in the city, he'd upset her more than once. But she gave back as good as she got, trying everything in her power to control the situation. When she had to give in, she'd done so in such a fashion, he'd never doubted her reluctance.

Now he understood so much, probably far more than she realized. Bethany's reactions, her attitudes, were completely predictable.

Her need to hide her femininity was under-standable. He could only wonder why she wasn't even more bitter.

She'd gone from apathetic to audacious, from submission to impertinence. Somewhere along the way, she'd also grown into the most fascinating woman he'd ever known. For all the good it would do him. There was no doubt she felt soiled by what had happened to her. Compared to his list of sins, Bethany's life had been one of utmost purity. It had been that day on the yacht, more than anything else, that had shown him how low his life had sunk.

After a while, giving up even the pretense of sleep, he quietly went about attempting to repair the damage done so long ago. By the time she began to stir, he was once again sitting near her.

❧❧

For once, the pretending must have worked. She drifted in and out of sleep for a while, her mind registering occasional back-ground noises that were soothing rather than unsettling. The sleep deepened, drawing her into the seductive darkness of non-thought, where memories could be temporarily ignored. Gradually, she was enticed out of her shell of false safety.

Her eyes burned from unshed tears. Muscles that had been clenched even as she dozed, ever prepared for flight, protested when she tried to straighten them. Worst of all were her throat and mouth. Dry and raw, they felt like she'd been running desperately through a desert.

All of these woes were not proof against the sounds and smells now slithering through the seams of her internal shelter. A quietly popping fire served as a counterpoint to even breathing that wove itself into her unconscious mind, easing some of her fears while she slept. Freshly brewed coffee, enhanced by an exotic liqueur, seduced her nostrils. Even as she registered the after effects of high drama in the middle of the night and questioned the incautious, perhaps even foolish, revelations, she rose to the bait like a trout starved for the sun.

Turning over became a struggle between muscles reluctant to obey and coverings determined to keep her pinned down. It took the dual seduction of coffee and an energetic fire to give her the energy to finish the maneuver. Only when she once more faced the room, attempting to raise herself against the pull of the covers, did she see her host, nemesis, and occasional friend.

He sat in front of the armchair, his lap and the floor around him covered with photographs. From time to time he shuffled through them but mostly he just sat, staring into the fire. A coffee mug on the floor near his leg couldn't be the source of the strong, enticing scent. Craning her head back slightly, she saw a similar mug on the table near the end of the couch. Fragrant steam rose seductively above it, drifting over to tease her. A glass of water was next to it, adorned with beads of moisture reflecting the firelight.

Just as she had decided that the contents of these would be well worth the effort needed to reach for them, Jonathan turned his head slightly. His expression was guarded and there was a curious stillness about him, as though he were braced for a confrontation. As this thought crossed her mind, one side of his mobile mouth quirked up, and he set the photos on his lap to one side.

"I thought that would be the best bait to entice you out," he said softly, rising to his knees.

His movements were the sort used around half wild creatures. It was irritating, but the lassitude remaining from her too brief, too deep sleep kept her from protesting before he had reached her side. By then it was too late.

"Be still. Let me help." His hands were as gentle as his voice. Deftly unwinding the quilts from around her legs until she had enough freedom to sit up, he supported her back until pillows could be stuffed behind her. Only then did he reach for the glass, forestalling her movements.

The water washed over her tongue, blessedly cool and refreshing. Once the glass was empty, Jonathan reached for the aromatic mug. It was fortunate he'd chosen to give in to his caretaking impulses. Although her hands were not shaking, Bethany found they held little of the strength she had come to depend upon. Not until a third of the hot, fortified, coffee had made its way down her throat was she able to hold the mug by herself. Only when he saw her fingers tighten and hold with purpose did Jonathan ease away from her, letting his weight rest on his heels.

"What—" her voice was as weak as her hands had been and she paused to clear her throat before trying again. "What are you doing still up? I told you I wouldn't go anywhere."

"I couldn't sleep anyway so I thought I'd keep the fire going." He kept his voice low, even.

Not letting his attention leave her face he leaned back, reaching for his own coffee. Her gaze followed the movement, going past his still, watchful face to the jumble of photos he'd set aside. She felt an unreasoning anger fill her.

"And look over your little collection, Mr. Merritt? How long have you hoarded mementoes of 'The Virgin Idiot'?" The earthenware mug was a victim of her emotions, propelled from her grasp to smash against the hearth when she flung out her arm, indicating the offensive photos.

"Have you been sitting here comparing your pictures to the real thing? Was that what all this was about?" Her voice rose with every question until she was almost screaming in his face.

"All what?" he snapped, his voice pinched with anger.

"All of this. Pretending you wanted an interview, getting me up here, being nice to me. Making me like you, dammit!"

"I don't believe you're for real. After all you've been through, how can you still be so naive!" He grabbed for her thrashing arms, fingers biting into her wrists with none of his usual care. "I didn't collect those damned pictures. I took them."

CHAPTER 9

The fire still announced its warmth with cheerful crackling. The scent of coffee and liqueur was stronger than ever from the liquid flung on the hot hearth. No doubt the earth still moved as it was supposed to upon its axis, and the stars continued in their proscribed orbits. These sorts of things wouldn't change just because an event of a cataclysmic nature had occurred in Bethany's life.

"You..." She hesitated, searching desperately for the right words. A slight tug released his grip on her wrists and she sat fully upright, bracing against the back of the couch, drawing her legs up closer to her body. "I don't remember seeing you there," she said in a lost little voice.

"You looked to be so drugged, I'm surprised you saw yourself, much less some stranger with a camera. I looked different, anyway."

Oh, yes, the drugs. *'Here dear, have a sip of this it will make you feel much better...Stefan is worried you'll be too nervous...take this, it's from the doctor. Wash it down with a sip of wine. That's the girl...'* Well-meaning voices, seeming so concerned for her welfare. All the while, they knew. Damn them, they knew. By the time she stood in front of that mob, wearing only that travesty of a wedding outfit, everything had been a blur.

"Did I ever meet you?"

꿍꿍

Her voice was small, muffled, her face hidden against her knees. Jonathan felt helpless. She seemed so fragile now, so lost, as though a master fiend had obliterated every point of reference from her life.

"I doubt it. I wasn't around much after the wedding, and I left Europe maybe six months later. Bethany—"

"What do you mean, you looked different?" She still sounded vague, distant, while she searched for topics to distract him. For now, Jonathan was willing to go along with her self-deception. This night had not only forced her to face her past, but also to allow it to be exposed to someone essentially still a stranger. He was sure the fact that he wanted to be far more wouldn't mean very much to her at the moment.

"Younger, and I dressed more like the people I photographed. Honey, are you all right?"

"Of course I'm all right. Why did you leave Europe?"

"I was tired of being there." How long would she sound so fragile? Would his patience, never a strong trait, last that long? Her brittle voice was frightening. "Bethany—"

"Did you take any wildlife pictures in Europe? There are some lovely areas in the Black Forest." Apparently, she thought as long as she concentrated on trivial subjects, and didn't meet his eyes, her voice could stay steady.

"The only pictures of wild life I took in Europe were on yachts and beaches," he said, his patience deserting him.

Bethany flinched, probably as much from his tone as from the memories his words must have brought back. Still, she kept her forehead resting on her knees, hugging her legs tightly against her chest. It was just as well. He wasn't quite ready to face the judgment he knew would be on her face.

"Did you...were you married to someone there?"

"Bethany!" His patience finally giving way, Jonathan clamped his fingers around her ankles, through the thick quilts, avoiding her injuries as he attempted to straighten out her legs.

She jumped, obviously not expecting his touch. For the first time her head lifted and she met his gaze steadily. Her eyes were endless pools of quiet pain, red rimmed, her eyelashes tangled from suppressed tears. She caught her lower lip between her teeth, biting down, probably to control any betraying tremble.

"Now, what did I tell you about that?" All traces of impatience were obliterated as he ran his hand slowly along the quilts, up her leg, across her arm, over her shoulder, to cup her chin. His thumb slid caressingly along her cheek, stroking an errant tear away from the corner of her eye before moving down to gently liberate her lip. For a brief moment he ran his thumb back and forth along her lower lip, savoring the soft fullness before drawing reluctantly away.

❧❧❧

Bethany found herself fighting for breath as completely foreign sensations shimmered through her body. She was supremely aware of his hand retracing the path back down her body to rest once more around her ankle. But she did not feel confined or pinned. Instead, she felt unsettled, drained, yet somehow also fulfilled.

Giving in to his gentle insistence, she allowed him to straighten her legs until they slid over the edge of the couch, quilts and all, and her feet were on the floor between his knees. Only then did he release his hold on her ankles, resting his forearms on her thighs and taking both of her cold hands between his much larger, much warmer ones. His touch offered warmth, friendship, and the promise of something more if she could just figure out how to ask for it.

❧❧❧

"Bethany," he began in a low voice, while his fingers stroked warmth into her bruised hands. "I will never be proud about the part I played in your wedding. Granted, I didn't know who you were, but I knew what was going on." It wasn't the total truth but it was as much truth as he dared tell her right then. "If you never want to talk about it, I won't care, but if you ever do need to talk about it, I'll be glad to listen. Alright?"

He looked up, searching her withdrawn face for the secrets she'd kept locked up for so long behind her fragile mask. No wonder she sometimes seemed like she was ready to fly into a million pieces. The miracle was that she'd survived as sanely as she had. When she nodded, even attempting a weak smile, he felt as though it were Christmas morning, and all the presents under the tree were for him.

"Now, you have yet to get enough sleep. Before I tuck you back in again, would you help me do something?"

She nodded again. When he tugged gently on her hands, she responded with utmost trust, sliding along the leather couch until she perched on the edge. Another soft pull as he backed away and she was kneeling on the thick hearth rug, edging closer to the fire.

Once she was off the couch and following his lead, Jonathan moved back to where he'd dropped the photos. He settled her next to him, pilfering pillows and quilts to make a soft, warm spot for her. It was an indication of how far they'd already come when she only protested briefly before settling down. They had light years still to go before they were as close as he wanted them to be.

"Here." He chose a photo at random, one of the entire wedding party in a giddy pose of bonhomie and inebriation, and pushed it into her hand. "Burn it."

"Do what?" Once she'd seen what was in the photo, she'd been reluctant even to touch the edges. But the idea of destroying the image was obviously so enticing, she ceased her protest and took the picture between two fingers.

"Burn it. Toss it into the fire. You know you want to do it." He watched her closely, seeing the gradual change as she realized what he gave her sanction to do. It would be a symbolic gesture, burning them in effigy. If it brought one moment's peace or happiness to her life, he would gladly let her torch his whole damned studio.

A small smile slowly softened her lips, tempting him beyond all ability to think. It was only a moment before light, both from within her and reflected from the fire, began to gleam in her eyes.

"Oh, yes, I want to do it." Her voice was stronger, richer, than it had been all evening. With no further thought she flexed her wrist, sending the picture deep into the hottest part of the fire.

Burn in hell, he thought, watching the self-important, over-indulged wastrels glisten, flicker, then melt into a puddle of charred chemicals. The photos followed one after another into the fire in an orgy of retribution. It was a fitting end for the images of people who had lived by the tenet that their wants were more important than anyone else's needs. Then he came to the first of the bridal pictures.

"You look so young," he murmured. "So incredibly, heart-wrenchingly young and innocent."

His photographs portrayed the bride all too faithfully. Short dark hair gamine cut by the stylist who had created the look, make-up applied by the hands of the genius whose company had taken three generations of women from beautiful to gorgeous. She held a lavish bouquet of rare miniature white orchids, picked deep in the rain forests of South America and flown in for this ceremony. The lace for her veil had been created by devout hands in a convent which had produced lacework of this gossamer perfection for centuries.

The veil was secured by a pearl crown that had belonged to a medieval princess. It framed a pensive face dominated by her hazy green eyes and lush, slightly trembling mouth, and billowed down to handmade, four inch spike heels. Delicate curves hinted at the woman she would one day become. The diaphanous covering enhanced her bridal outfit, personally designed by the hand of the dresser to royalty. Tiny, white fire opals had been meticulously applied to the hand sewn, French cut white bikini.

Jonathan stared blindly at his work, re-membering that day more clearly than he wanted to. From memory came the feel of the deck rolling gently under his feet, the all-pervasive sea-scented air. The elite of the world's "beautiful people," a few hundred of Dubec's closest, most personal friends, crowded the yacht, reveling in the drama taking place in front of them. Then Bethany's voice, soft, hesitant, brought him back to the present—and reality.

"I had my seventeenth birthday a month later. I was an exceptionally good student. They let me graduate early." She said it matter-of-factly, but not all the ghosts were going up the chimney with the smoke.

Sixteen years old. He'd known, of course, that she had been extremely young. That had been the major attraction. But, sixteen? "I remember when my sisters turned sixteen, and got their driver's licenses." As he spoke he stared into the fire, seeking memories. "I used to listen to them jabber. The most they ever had to worry about was drive-in movies, a wet kiss from a date and what dress they were going to wear to the prom."

"Jonathan, don't. It wasn't your fault. Anyway, I survived, didn't I?"

He closed his eyes briefly, wondering how badly the total truth would hurt their relationship, and reluctant to find that out now.

Blindly, he reached for the next set of pictures on the pile, opening his eyes only enough to ensure his aim.

"'Far, far better thing I do...'" The voice from near his shoulder was a sleepy murmur, rich with memories both sad and lovely. The sound was so gentle, so poignant, he straightened in time to see the yacht, under full sail, going up in flames along with the scantily clad child-woman it had been named after.

"What do you mean, honey?" He pitched his voice to the same low tone.

"Like the end of *Tale of Two Cities*. Daddy's gorgeous boat blew up. They said it was an accident with the propane. I had enough from the insurance to get away. He really did love me, but after Mama died he was so lost." Her words faded as she succumbed to the day and the hour. As though acting of its own volition, her head leaned toward him, coming to rest on his shoulder. "Jonathan?"

"Yes, Bethany." His breath was a whisper against her scalp as he dared to place a kiss on her temple.

"I've never been to a drive-in. Could we go someday?"

He shifted, settling her more comfortably against his side. His arm came naturally around her shoulders and she was too tired, or too comfortable, to protest.

"We can do anything you want to, honey. Would you like the chance to be a teenager?"

"That sounds like fun." Her voice was almost too low to be heard, but the next words engraved themselves on what was left of his heart. "Jonathan, will you stay with me again tonight? I don't think I want to be alone."

Bringing his other arm around, he dared a light hug, and secured her now definitely sleeping form against his side. "Don't worry, precious. You won't ever be alone again."

Sleep would not come to Jonathan for a long time that night. Eyes burning from exhaustion and smoke, face set in grim lines, he held Bethany and watched Lulu become only a memory. All too often, the images he saw were not the ones he was destroying.

∽✺∾

Stockinged feet propped on the hassock, Bethany looked over the yellow legal pad. Stacks of paper in various colors surrounded her, with scraps added here and there, either stuck on or attached by bright plastic clips. She glanced out the window, seeing the words in her head instead of the beautiful morning outside. Tapping her pen against her lower lip, she made a few notes on the page in front of her then turned to a blank page.

"I thought I told you not to start any work until you were better."

The stern voice commanded from the hallway, which was raised a few feet above the living room area. Scribbling furiously, Bethany merely waved one hand in acknowledgement. When he stepped further in the room, she raised her hand, demanding silence until she could commit her thought to paper. Jonathan settled quietly in the large chair, apparently summoning patience until she looked up.

"Your exact words were, as I recall, you would 'not answer any damned questions until I was feeling better.' However, your interview is not the only piece I can work on."

He laughed softly, leaning back in what seemed to be total comfort and studying her over his steepled fingers.

"I was under the impression Chandler delayed everything to give you time up here."

"Interviews, yes." She set the yellow pad down and stretched her legs, pushing the hassock in his direction in case he wanted to relax further. Immediately, Jonathan lifted his moccasined feet onto the opposite edge of the leather stool. It had a comfortable, homey feeling to it. "I wanted to frame out something else so that I would be ready before I got there."

"The shelter story?" He nodded along with her. "What's so fascinating about that place?"

"Other than the fact that they've completely turned around the lives of women who had nowhere else to go?" She knew her tone had become a shade hostile, then she caught the same small smile on Jonathan's face she'd seen in Neil's office. He was testing her, pushing subtly to see how far she would go before she caught on.

"Other than that," he said blandly, once he realized she wasn't going to bite.

"Most shelters offer a refuge for women and children to stay when they have nowhere else to go," she explained in the patient tone used on feeble minds. "They're wonderful, and they really fill a need. At this one, in addition to living space and emotional support, they encourage learning marketable trade skills or furthering education, so the women don't have to feel dependent." She dropped her feet to the floor, leaning over to search among the papers.

"Here." She showed him a typed list, with hand-written additions. "These are some of the women who've gone on from there. They've become environmental experts, teachers, artists, designers. A couple of them are pre-med, and one's at UC Davis, going into her last year of vet school. A lot of the ones who don't choose college have successful careers, because they've learned they can take care of themselves. This place gives them a real sense of self-worth."

He took the list, but didn't look at it right away. Instead, he looked at her, a slight frown furrowing his brow. There was a new light in his blue eyes, softer yet somehow more intense, as though he were thinking deep thoughts at a frantic rate. Then he leaned forward, resting his elbows on his knees.

"How long did it take you to learn 'a real sense of self-worth,' Bethany?"

She flushed, turning away, a bit embarrassed by the passion of her speech. Keeping her face averted, she began gathering up the papers, putting them in order in a file folder. When she had the spot next to her cleared, Jonathan moved out of the chair and sat down. He did it so quickly, she didn't have a chance to move before he was next to her, his weight depressing the couch, his heat flowing along her side.

With one hand, he removed the papers from her hand, setting them on the hassock. His other hand moved up to touch her gently on the neck. Stroking up to her chin, he urged her to raise her face until she was forced to meet his eyes.

"Who was there for you, Bethany, when you left Europe with no marketable educational skills and very little money? Did you have any family to take you in?"

"My mother's family disowned her when she married my father and I never did figure out exactly where his family came from. M. Armand, my father's lawyer, tried to find someone, but he gave up eventually. Instead, he got in touch with a hostel in Virginia. They gave me somewhere to stay while I got my bearings and got rid of my accent."

"I thought I recognized a bit of a Southern drawl there." He continued to stroke her neck, wakening feelings she hadn't known she possessed. His breath stirred the hairs along her temple, warming instead of threatening. "You want to write this article to give something back to the people who were there for you, don't you? No, don't shrug. I can understand you wanting to give back what was given to you."

He stroked her neck briefly, but she didn't find it in herself to be nervous. There'd been too many instances of trust between them. Almost reluctantly, he slid his fingers along to the covered safety of her shoulder, and squeezed gently.

"There's a beautiful morning out there, going to waste," he said bracingly, as if wanting to pacify her nervous qualms. "It looks like your energy, at least, needs to get some jeans and shoes on and go out for a while."

She leapt up, using her ankle carefully so he wouldn't change his mind. There was only a minor twinge, which would quickly work out. At the doorway, she hesitated.

"Don't worry, I didn't throw out those wretched rags you insist on wearing," he assured her, but there was an oddly satisfied note in his voice.

⁓⁓⁓

Watching the too enticing derriere in front of him, Jonathan made a mental note to commend Marsha Chandler's taste and sensitivity. Bethany would not have been happy in jeans that fit the way jeans were meant to fit. Even so, the change in costume made enough of a difference in her appearance to have a dangerous effect on the self-control he'd once taken for granted. All of this ran through his mind as he watched her navigate a portion of the trail in front of him.

It hadn't been easy, talking with her earlier that morning. Bethany without her prickly exterior and impenetrable walls was a dangerous person to have around. Her growing trust was a strange and very potent aphrodisiac.

She'd seemed surprised when he encouraged her to dress, until she realized that the only clothes available were those supplied by Neil's wife. She glared at him suspiciously when he said there hadn't been time to wash anything.

When she emerged from the bedroom, her wild hair confined by bands on either side of her chin, a smile softened her eyes if not her mouth. Her slender silhouette drew his eyes but he merely extended a hand, refraining from comment. He'd found, after several false starts, that she would allow him to touch her, to help her heal, if he remembered to talk to her first, and didn't surprise her. It was an easy plan to follow, especially as every day brought a lessening of the deep-rooted distrust Bethany had learned at the hands of her husband.

Thinking about this made him clench his jaw, and brought again the fear that all the truths would have to be revealed before she could learn not every man was like the ones she'd known. He consciously relaxed himself, deciding to let the days happen as they would. Right now, at this instant, Bethany trusted him and seemed happy. He would build on that.

"Hey, slow down up there. I've been slaving away while you've been resting up. Have pity on me."

Bethany paused, looking back over her shoulder. A near smile lit her eyes, almost lifting the corners of her soft mouth. He realized he'd never seen her smile, and he desperately wanted that from her. She'd put on another one of her damned caps, but left her hair down to lay along her shoulders, almost touching the rise of her breasts beneath the navy over-shirt.

"Well, get a move on, Grandpa. We're burning daylight here." The rough colloquialism, in her elegant voice, was delightfully paradoxical.

"I've been meaning to ask where you acquired your distinctive speech mannerisms," he asked, manfully stifling his grin.

"Here and there. I've interviewed people who were as individualistic in their speech as they were in life-style."

He noticed again how she lit up when she talked about her work. She forgot about herself and became a complete, confident person when she wrote. It was a fascinating metamorphosis, a critical clue to her overall personality.

"You like your job, don't you?" He joined her on a ridge, overlooking an area they hadn't explored.

"I've enjoyed it," she answered seriously, looking over the valley while she formed her thoughts. "The people I find aren't world leaders, but they have so much to offer and no one has ever asked for it before. Some of them dropped out intentionally, some just grew out of the habit of communicating. Once I can convince them of how special they are, they open up and share with me. When they agree to the interview it's usually because, deep down inside, they're tired of the isolation, and want to be found again."

"Like me?"

"Well, if the shoe fits..." she let her voice trail off suggestively.

"It's probably the wrong color."

"Cynic." But there was no rancor in her voice. "I like to think that, by presenting these people and the world to each other, I help translate for them. All too often, people are misunderstood because no one ever took the time to understand who they are, or what they're saying behind the surface words."

Jonathan felt that twinge again, that unexpected ache deep inside him that had come and gone so often in the last few days. How many, he asked her silently, had understood the frightened girl behind the obscene virgin persona? How many even tried? *And what did you do about it, Merritt? Did you rush to the rescue, snatch her away from the evil moneylender, protect her from the world because she couldn't protect herself?* Not hardly.

"Jonathan, are you all right? You look odd."

"Just exhausted. You wore me out with your constant demands for attention." He managed to say it lightly, pushing the words past the lump of guilt in his chest. "Are you up to more of a hike, or am I going to have to carry you back again?"

"You are too generous, kind sir," she said with another near smile, her green eyes glinting. With her hair pulled to the sides and fluffing out below the bands, she looked younger than ever, and extremely vulnerable.

Unable to stop himself, without thinking first, Jonathan reached out to touch one of those clumps of hair, to push it behind her shoulder and expose the elegance of her neck. Without seeming to avoid his touch, she moved away within herself, turning to follow a gently sloping trail down into the wilderness valley. The moment passed without stress, leaving him more on edge than before.

"How does your family feel about your work?" she asked over her shoulder. "We've never really discussed that." The impersonal question helped defuse the moment. He chose to go along with her lead.

"At first they couldn't decide how they felt about it. It's not as though I have a real job, like photographing babies at the mall, or something equally redeeming. Once the first book sold, they began to accept my work a little more. It was only when I had a calendar come out a couple years ago they finally thought I might make a go of it."

"They must be very proud of you."

"Oh, yeah. They have my book out on display right next to my brother's state fair prize for zucchini."

"But that's wonderful!" At his snort, she rushed on, daring to grab his sleeve to get his full attention. "Don't you understand? They're honoring the achievements of both of their children."

"I would like to think that my book was a greater achievement than an oversized squash." He maintained the superior tone with an effort. Her fleeting touch had set off alert signals that were interfering with his brain relays.

"Perhaps in some minds. Your book would not be nearly as tasty cooked in a marinara sauce and topped with cheese."

She was teasing him. She was actually opening up to him, letting her dangerous lips tilt up at the corners and part in a for-real smile. Her fingers had left his arm but the essence of her touch was closer than ever, enticing him with an unconscious siren's song. Mindful of her reaction, he lifted his hand to remove a leaf that had nested in her hair.

"It looks like you're going to have to be groomed just like Baron when we get back."

"That's why I kept my hair up."

"Since you're always so busy grooming Baron, how about I take charge of your hair?"

He tried to make it sound like the most natural thing in the world. Bethany glanced at him from under her lashes, as if remembering in spite of herself the comfort and pleasure she'd received from his hands in her hair. The offer might not seem to be in keeping with the kind of person she had once thought he was, but it was the kind of thing a friend might like to do for her.

"Okay." This time her smile lit up his world.

CHAPTER 10

S o, where do we hike today, scout leader?" Bethany produced a tiny grin as she asked from her spot seated on the deck. Jonathan had decided she needed to experience teenage activities. By his definition, this included the Girl Scouts. They drew the line at braiding lanyards, leaf collections, and camping out. But every moment of every day had been crammed with platonic activity.

Sometimes they stayed in. Jonathan worked in his darkroom and answered Bethany's questions, helping to fill out the framework she'd developed for the interview. Dinners were casual, with Jonathan doing most of the cooking. Particularly after he proposed a special merit badge for one meal produced completely free of charred spots.

Bethany couldn't explain why she displayed even less than her normal mediocre talent in the kitchen. She didn't think it was intimidation because he was so competent.

Perhaps the lapses in attention, which caused her to forget what she was doing, had to do with her tendency to suddenly notice, or remember, how special Jonathan was to be around.

Certainly her occasional moments of breathlessness had nothing to do with the fact that Jonathan touched her all the time. Not intimate touches or anything that could embarrass her. But he was forever laying a hand on her shoulder as he reached for something in the cupboard over her head. Or throwing his arm across her shoulders when they were looking at something. Friendly touches. Casual touches. Certainly nothing to let herself be flustered over.

"Suggestions, Bwana?" Jonathan's mouth quirked up in the maddening twist he achieved whenever he was enjoying himself. In deference to the unseasonable warmth, he was comfortably dressed in a short sleeved shirt, walking shorts and low boots. His legs, lean and lightly covered in dark hair, were certainly not why she had difficulty looking at him while they spoke.

"It is warm enough to be on safari." she grimaced, attempting to blot the moisture already collecting on the edge of her hairline.

"You can't blame all your discomfort on the weather, Bethany. The layered look is not really a fashion statement this season."

"Shows you how much I've kept up on that sort of thing." She very intentionally kept her voice light, airy.

Moving deliberately, he leaned down to rest his hands on her shoulders.

"Bethany. Look at me. That's right. You have the most amazing eyes. Like a deep forest glade," he said, his voice seemingly casual. "It's unusually warm today, and muggy. You go out like that, you run the risk of heatstroke. Let me loan you a pair of shorts."

"I'm fine. I've worn this in the desert in the summertime." One time, and she'd suffered a particularly noxious heat rash because of it. After that, she scheduled her desert assignments for the winter.

"Bethany, Bethany." He sighed, rocking her from side to side. "You must realize by now nothing is going to happen if you remove a few layers around me."

221

She stared at him, feeling her eyes widen. How could she explain to him she almost wanted something to happen? The man had offered his home and his privacy to her. He certainly wasn't interested in the illogical reactions of a warped female whose emotions had been put on hold ten years previously. She was sure the strange sensations that were so unsettling they sometimes interfered with her sleep had to do only with said emotions finally stirring to life. Not with her reaction to one particular person.

"It's–I know I can trust you, it's just..." She had to resort to a shrug, feeling an odd tingling in her eyes.

Jonathan slid his hands slowly down her arms, stepping away to give her more space while he lightly held her hands.

"It's all right, Bethany. Wear whatever you want. We'll just make it a short walk this morning, anyway. I want to get some morning pictures of the stream on the north hill to go with the afternoon and evening shots. I need to go into town today to check on the mail. Want to come along?"

Pulling away from his gentle grasp, Bethany turned to follow Baron down the rough-hewn steps. She stopped at the bottom, looking back up to watch Jonathan, wondering how long he was going to put up with her irrational fears. He'd been unfailingly polite, no matter how violently she jerked away when she felt crowded. The enforced proximity would eventually have a negative effect on him. Maybe an afternoon apart would help.

"Thanks, but I think I'll stay here and knock around some ideas."

He merely grunted an acknowledgement. But she knew, from the look in his eyes, that he understood even better than she did why she didn't want to go to town with him.

৫৩৫৩

Jonathan didn't allow himself to relax until he was rolling back up his driveway in the ancient but very serviceable Willys Jeep. It had seemed a calculated risk to leave her alone for the afternoon. After her abortive attempt to run away rather than admit who she was, he'd replaced the keys in the motorhome. Whether she stayed or left would be totally up to her, and he wouldn't argue with her decision either way. Even so, he expelled a deep breath he hadn't realized he was holding when he saw the battered vehicle still nestled among the trees. She'd decided to stick it out a little longer.

His relief was short-circuited when he spotted the small import truck behind the motorhome. Apparently Bethany had had company while he was gone. He tried to reminded himself that it could be, probably was, work-related. Past history, and his experiences with his wife, had taught him more cynicism than trust.

He braked the Jeep next to the motorhome, no longer feeling an insane urge to sweep through the front door of the house, calling: "Honey, I'm home!" He doubted Bethany had memories of classic American television, anyway.

Instead, he let himself into the house quietly, stopping inside the front door to listen before carrying his packages into the kitchen. His sunglasses darkened the empty rooms but he could navigate the house blindfolded. The delicate precision of Strauss filled the rooms. There was a murmur of voices in the direction of the deck, and Baron slipped through the partially opened glass door to greet him with quiet glee. He followed the wagging red tail back onto the deck, and stopped before he could step through the door and make a total fool of himself.

She'd pinned up her hair to keep it off her neck while she worked, but for once he couldn't complain. The upswept hair revealed her long slender neck, and shoulders of such elegant beauty they could have well graced the body of a seventeenth century courtesan. A loose tank top, bright blue, exposed the pale perfection of skin untouched by the sun for years. For the first time Jonathan understood the Victorian philosophy of revealing limited amounts of bare flesh. After so long of seeing only loose, encompassing coverings in dark, drab colors, the expanse of skin was instantly arousing.

Leaning against the deck railing was the young photographer Jonathan had met in San Francisco. He looked out over the trees, commenting on something he'd apparently just seen. Bethany was looking through something on her lap, paying Casey only minimal attention. The bare tinge of pink at the base of her neck, and the over-shirt discarded near her chair, attested to the fact that she hadn't been uncovered for long. If there was anything going on here besides work, it wasn't romance. Still, he didn't like it.

Jonathan felt like a second rate spy, and wondered how he could reveal himself without letting them know he'd been watching. Stepping back into the kitchen he poured himself some juice, and returned to the door, being sure to knock into a chair on his way.

"You were smart to stay here. I can't remember when it's been such a hot and dusty drive. But it was worth it." As he spoke, Jonathan stepped out onto the deck and around the lounge chair she was sitting in. Both of them looked up, expressions of innocent greeting on their faces. Bethany almost seemed relieved, the few seconds her eyes would meet his.

"Good afternoon, Casey. Something to drink? I picked up some juice in our thriving metropolis." He lifted the glass, a question obvious in his raised eyebrows, but accepted their refusal without comment. He leaned on the rail near the younger man, looking out over the trees himself and wondering how many millennia it would be before he could breathe properly and regain control of his bodily responses.

Her back had been lovely but the brief glimpse of her front was enough to teach him prayer. The looseness of her top only served to outline and emphasize full round breasts. He could almost believe he saw a hint of a nipple, but that might only be wishful thinking. He had also seen the uncertainty in her face, though she seemed to welcome his presence. It would take very little to send her back into hiding. Certainly giving in to the black rage that continued to threaten wouldn't do any good.

"I hope it's all right that I dropped by without calling, Mr. Merritt. Acton wanted to see the photos as soon as I got them and I was coming up this direction anyway, sort of and..." Casey colored, stammering into silence when Jonathan made no further response than a lifted eyebrow.

"It's no problem, Casey." Bethany filled in the silence while she gathered the photos she'd been going through. "These look really good. You caught the emphasis I want to use, of how high these women are going, not just how low they were."

It was a courteous re-direction of the subject, no doubt drilled into her at the schools she'd attended. Jonathan knew the curricula covered much of life's unpleasantness. Whatever the origin, her gracious words helped eliminate the discomfort caused by his absurd reactions. Casey basked in her mild praise, moving away from the rail to point out something in one of the photos.

Bethany rose smoothly, setting down the envelope of photos and reaching for her over shirt. Without making a big production of it, she had her arms in the sleeves and her back covered before Casey could move a step closer. By the time the young photographer was at her side, she once more held the envelope; using it like a shield in front of her while she buttoned her shirt one-handed.

෴

"Casey, I didn't realized you two had met." Over-shirt buttoned, Bethany felt more comfortable facing the world. When she'd decided to try exposing her skin to the air, she'd thought she would hear Jonathan's Jeep returning. Instead, Casey appeared around the corner of the house, having followed the sound of the music. There hadn't been a chance to cover up without feeling like a total fool. Not that Casey mattered, or for that matter noticed.

When Jonathan walked out onto the deck, she was glad to have the photos to pretend to be looking at. Why did she feel so much less dressed around him? Jonathan had glanced at her, briefly, before turning to talk with Casey. It was nothing more than a polite, friendly look. She certainly didn't want anything else.

"We met in the city, the morning after our pizza bash," Casey was saying as he reached for the envelope in Bethany's hands. "You two had coffee in Chandler's office later, remember?"

There wasn't much she could forget about that day. Apparently, Jonathan's thoughts were not pleasant. He scowled, finishing the juice and setting the glass down solidly on the railing. Something in the trees had obviously caught his attention.

"I believe she chose that morning to sleep in," he reminded Casey, not bothering to turn around again.

"Probably. She looked pretty beat by the time I left." Casey was sorting through the photos, pointing out his favorites. He didn't bother to look up when the glass shattered on the deck, so he missed Jonathan's scowl. When Bethany stepped toward the house, intending to get a broom and dustpan, she was waved back by a peremptory hand.

"I'll take care of it. You stay with your guest."

Jonathan seemed almost angry, as though he minded Casey's visit. She knew her young friend had an elastic view of manners, but it seemed odd that Jonathan would react so extremely. It wasn't as though Casey was bothering anything.

"Do you want to keep any of these? I made some extra copies." Oblivious as ever, Casey was still enthralled by his work. "Some of these women were pretty amazing, Acton. Do you realize how little most of them started out with?"

"That was the whole idea of getting Neil to approve the article, remember?" Some things never changed, including the need to continue small talk when all you wanted to do was go somewhere else. "What are you working on now, that brought you up here?"

For once, Casey looked slightly chagrined. He shrugged, sliding the photos back into the envelope and fastening the string clasp.

"How about I leave these all with you? I have pretty much a full set for myself."

"Casey, did Neil send you up here to check on me?" The suspicion was ugly, but she had to know.

"No." Casey was firm in his denial. "Neil sort of thinks I'm in Sacramento, checking on the railroad museum. I figured, since this was so close..." He shrugged, his voice trailing off.

"Four hours isn't 'close,' Casey. What's up? And while I'm thinking about it, how did you find this place?"

Now the young photographer allowed himself a small, superior smile. "My older brother was in one of those activist groups for a while, before he decided to become a CPA. He always told me to collect your own information if you really want to know what's going on. When I found out Merritt lived in Northern California, I got a friend to check the tax records for the general area."

"For goodness sakes, why?"

231

"Hell, Acton, you said it in your review. He's just about the greatest photographer since Adams or Stieglitz. I thought maybe I could, you know, take a vacation up here sometime and accidently bump into him at the store or something. I never dreamed he'd actually invite you here for a while."

"You thought you'd trade on our friendship?" Bethany felt a familiar sort of sadness.

"Pretty sick, huh?" He blushed, looking far younger than his twenty-five years. "I'm sorry, Acton. I know how you feel about your privacy."

"That's all right, Casey. I guess if you can't take advantage of your friends, what's left in the world? You want him to look at some of your work while you're here?"

"No," he said, looking suddenly more mature. "I'll talk to him at a gallery, or drop him a letter. If you want I can just put your copies in your rig on my way out. It's not locked, is it?"

"Of course not, but do you have to rush off?"

"He's got at least an hour's drive on unfamiliar roads before he hits the freeway," Jonathan said, directly behind her. "It's best he doesn't wait until it's dark." His voice held no welcome.

Casey took the hint immediately, stopping only to pat Baron before he leapt off the porch. In the act of waving casually, his attention suddenly focused on Bethany.

"Acton, you look different somehow." He squinted, tilting his head as he looked up, then grinned. "Oh, yeah. Where's your hat?" Without waiting for a reply, he waved again and disappeared around the corner of the house.

"How long have you known him?" Jonathan asked, his tone strange as he came up to stand beside her.

"Since I started with *Western Living*, about five years. Why?"

"Is he always so unobservant?"

"Casey rarely notices anything unless he's looking through a camera lens. It's part of his deadly charm."

The quirky smile Jonathan used when he teased her was threatening to take over his lips. "How deadly is this charm?"

"Obviously not too much. He's trying to date a pre-med student who's more interested in cadavers than his living body. I guess it's really frustrating for him."

"I can imagine."

"Jonathan," Bethany began, feeling nervous, but determined. "You seemed upset when you first came in. Were you angry because Casey came by?"

He seemed to briefly consider trying one of the polite little lies people used when they've made fools of themselves but don't want anyone to know.

"At first, I wondered if you had called Casey when you found out I wouldn't be here this afternoon. It's something my wife would have done."

"Why?" Bethany asked, and then blushed slightly at her naiveté. "Why would she invite someone like Casey? He's a wonderful photographer, but he doesn't seem to do too well in relationships."

"That wasn't the point. Marlene wasn't happy unless she was causing trouble or someone was telling her how beautiful she was."

"Was she beautiful?" she asked, strolling over to look at the trees everyone else had found so fascinating.

"I must have thought so at some point. You may have seen her. Dark hair, standard well-kept jet set figure."

"Stefan didn't encourage me to socialize with his friends. I was simply supposed to parade in front of them from time to time, whenever he wanted to display his possessions." She regretted the bitterness of her tone, but it was difficult to speak more carefully.

How could this Marlene have been unhappy, if Jonathan thought enough of her to offer marriage? She glanced over at the man who joined her at the railing. To have the lean, tough elegance of this man in your bed every night and not be happy was impossible to comprehend. Feeling the heat rise in her face, she turned away.

"I think Marlene may have known Dubec for years," he said, "She probably should have married him but at that time he wanted a young bride."

Bethany shuddered, turning away abruptly. Before she could come near an escape, he took a gentle hold of her arm.

"Did you get much done on your article?"

"A fair amount. Actually, I had some ideas about the interview I wanted to frame out while they were still fresh."

"Good, then you're finished for today. Take this."

He handed her a dust pan to hold while he carefully swept the glass together. Fortunately, it had broken into larger pieces and was easily gathered up. "Are you in the mood for a Western, or would you like some light comedy? All classics, of course."

"What are you talking about?" She tried to sound remote, but was too intrigued. After the intense discussion about his wife, Jonathan was alert, cheerful, and something had him almost effervescing. It was a welcome change.

"You don't remember about the drive-in? You promised to take me!"

There was very little about that night she did not remember, whether she wanted to or not. But that statement sounded just a little bit off.

"I promised?"

"I knew you would forget!"

"You must have been a truly obnoxious child," she said, with an attempt at severity. "You have that whine down pat."

236

"None worser. I wasn't sure what you would like, so I got a variety. Do you have any preferences?"

Bethany tilted her head back, attempting to make eye contact through his tinted lenses. "You picked up films because I'd never been to a drive-in movie? Isn't that a bit excessive?"

Jonathan's toneless whistle was loud enough to be irritating. He chose to ignore her question. At last she stepped away from the railing, reaching for the materials she'd stashed under her chair when Casey showed up. Instantly the notebook and papers were removed to a place inside. They were replaced by a box of DVD cartridges.

"If I pick out a movie, will we shine the image on the trees so we can sit in a car?"

"Since I have a perfectly good wide screen, that would be silly. We can watch the movies in the living room and let our imaginations do the rest."

✂✁✂

"There are, of course, certain rules one must obey when attending a drive-in movie with one's date," Jonathan said in a mock serious voice while setting up the movies.

"Other than the fact that you never eat the food at a drive-in because it was made two years ago and frozen and it costs too much anyway?" Bethany stood by the couch where she'd been told to wait, clutching a bowl of popcorn. In deference to their age, Jonathan had selected coffee rather than soft drinks, and had set the tray with mugs and a carafe on a low table.

"Very good, you were paying attention." He flashed her a quick smile before punching the final buttons and picking up the remote control. While the screen lit up, revealing test patterns and FBI warnings, he pulled the pillows from the couch. The table on one side and hassock on the other roughly defined the front seat of a small car. They were settled, drinks distributed, as the credits began to roll for the main feature.

"What are we watching, anyway?" After an exhaustive discussion of the films available, Jonathan had decided to make the choice himself, due to his far greater experience.

"Ah, Rule Number One: The movie is not what is important, although spooky or mushy movies are more effective. What matters is the company. This brings us immediately to Rule Number Two: At least one person in the vehicle must be aware of what the movie is all about. Parents always want to know. It's a sneaky way of making sure you actually went to the movie."

"What else—"

"Hush. Watch the movie."

She subsided, recognizing the look of mischief on his face, and knowing he would be serious only when he felt like it. There hadn't been opportunity for her to see many movies, and she quickly found herself drawn into the plot of an upper-middle class young man who graduates from college and can't quite figure out what to do with himself.

The story was well presented, and she found herself concentrating on the film, only looking away to absently push Baron's nose out of the popcorn. Then Jonathan yawned hugely, stretching his hands over his head. When he lowered his arms, one of them came to rest along her shoulders, his long fingers lightly stroking her upper arm.

"Easy, honey. This is called: 'Putting a make on her while pretending you need more room.' Like so many classic maneuvers, it never really goes out of style."

"I see," she said dryly, forcing her body to ignore the sparks radiating from the contact of his arm on her neck. She'd put on a gray soft cotton sweater over the blue shell, but it was part of the clothing provided by Marsha, and had a loose cowl collar. One side drooped and she could feel the individual hairs on his forearm against her neck. "And is there a correct classic response for the one moved upon?"

This brought a snicker, and his other arm slid across the front of her body in a quick hug. Before she could decide if she wanted to protest, she was released.

"Any response is correct as long as the arm remains in position."

"Doesn't this eventually have a detrimental effect upon said arm?"

"No price is too great. Pay attention to the movie. That older woman is putting the make on the young guy."

She managed to absorb a few scenes before the stroking of his fingers through the soft cotton sweater became too distracting. An unconscious relaxation of her major muscles caused her to lean, ever so slightly, into the shelter of his body. When he spoke, his breath stirred the hairs that fallen around her ear.

"Of all possible responses, that is the best one. Just relax, Bethany. Feel good."

They watched the movie, or pretended to, as his hand idly moved on her arm. Sometimes the fingers would come almost to the drooping neckline of her sweater, where it had started to fall off her shoulder. Her skin would tingle in anticipation of a touch that never occurred. Then again, sometimes the fingers stroked down, cupping around her elbow, coming perilously close to a breast that was suddenly too swollen for the confinement of a sports bra. She squirmed, feeling a twinge lower in her body and not sure what to do about it.

With a soft murmur of approval Jonathan shifted, bringing his other arm back across her body in a loose embrace while his face nestled in the curve of her neck. A gradual tightening of his grip brought her closer until their sides melded from knee to shoulder. One knee lifted slightly over her thigh as his body shifted to half cover hers.

"At this point, I mention how tired I am. It's a great way to put a girl at ease. If I'm tired, I can't possibly be any danger to her. Then I mention how restful she is. That really gets to her, makes her feel all womanly and soft."

"And, am I restful?" she asked, in a hesitant voice, not wanting to sound too hopeful, but willing to play the game for a little while longer.

"The best. And womanly. And so soft," he whispered against her neck, and touched his lips ever so lightly to the warm satin skin behind her ear.

Feeling so much, yearning for something she didn't recognize, Bethany abandoned the inconsequential problems of the movie. Her eyes slitted, shutting out most of the dim light, while the muscles in her neck failed her completely and her head lolled to one side. His breath whispered over the skin behind her ear, tantalizing, promising unknown wonders. Then a warm, moist touch traced along the edges of her ear, and teeth closed ever so gently on the lobe, tugging, then releasing.

A long fingered hand, slightly calloused, came up to cradle her chin, supporting her, keeping her from dissolving into a puddle of overheated sensation. Unsure, at a total loss and wanting so much to respond, to give back a minor portion of the aching, shivering, glittering shower of feelings he was drenching her in, she nestled against the hand. For a very brief, very bold instant, she turned her head, and breathed a shy kiss into his palm.

Jonathan tensed like a sprinter braced for the run of his life. His arms contracted, turning her slightly as he shifted to come even closer, until they half lay, breast to aching breast, only the couch keeping them upright.

His knee began to develop wandering tendencies, bringing their lower bodies into more intimate contact. Bethany felt his urgent male heat against her thigh. This was something she knew. This heat, and the hand migrating down her arm, across her chest, attempting small soothing circles as it sought a nesting place. His upper body raised, beginning to come across hers. There was no sweet mystery in this. Jonathan wanted her body. Now.

The abrupt chilling shudder that raced through her stiffened her whole body and Jonathan pulled back, gulping lungsful of air.

His arms relaxed, hands soothed, encouraging her to nestle against him. Even in the sudden rush of fearful memories, she could accept his comfort.

It had been a close thing this time. She'd been opening up, responding to him in so many ways. But it was again too much, too soon, and he gave them both time to regroup.

"Then you back off because you can't let it go too far in public. Not if you have any respect for your date." He slid the fingers of his left hand along her neck, lightly stroking the tumultuous pulse beneath her heated skin.

A stroke along her cheek encouraged her to rest her forehead against his neck, until he could settle his chin in the fresh scent of her hair. "You watch the movie, because someone is bound to ask about it tomorrow, and you'll want to be able to answer them."

She tried to watch the movie. She really did. But chills, or fever spells, were tightening, stroking, attacking muscles and nerve endings she hadn't known she possessed. The brief flash of mistrust had passed but she was still shaking. Her hands were clenched together and she actually found herself wringing them, rubbing them along her arms to try to rid herself of the restless feelings.

Then Jonathan's hand descended on hers, surrounding her in warmth. His arm subtly tightened and loosened in a quick half hug of her shoulders while his thumb stroked along the tense tendons of her hands.

"You're going to overload on teenage experiences." In contrast to his airy words, his voice sounded as tense as her throat felt. Still, his hands were gentle, and he was very careful to keep their lower bodies from touching too intimately. A breath whispered along her forehead before his lips touched, so briefly, on her temple. "Welcome to the wonderful world of frustration."

CHAPTER 11

The eagle had finished its morning errands and was on the homeward commute, rising up convenient thermals to its nest. With its departure there were more birds in open sight, and enough small animals had come out of hiding to fulfill all of Baron's fantasies. Had the setter been human he would have been hurt to realize the animals feared a bird far more than they feared him. Being only a dog, he took his pleasures however they came, and was glad for them.

Bethany sat on a hollowed-out boulder, resting her shoulders against the sun-warmed granite. The early morning rays poured over her, touching skin bared by the open flannel over-shirt. Rich soil and pungent pine enticed her nostrils, tempting her to walk though she didn't have the energy that morning.

She'd been there for over an hour, and was not yet sure when she would head back. Certainly not before she'd had time for a lengthy discussion with herself, one she had yet to initiate. It would be nice, she often thought, to be a dog and be able to find pleasure in life's small offerings. Wanting, hurt so much.

"I thought I'd find you here." The voice was a gentle intrusion, an extension of the scuffling footsteps she'd been hearing. It was a kindly game he played, making noises as he approached, when she knew how silently he could move. "You left before breakfast."

"I wasn't really—" Turning as she spoke, she was stopped by the open thermos of coffee. Only then did she realize the rich aroma had been intruding on the forest scents for the last few minutes. A heavy plastic mug was pushed into her hands and filled with coffee.

"You always seem to be taking care of me. Why do you suppose that is?" Her voice was remote, as though the answer really didn't matter.

"Perhaps because someone has to. You keep forgetting to take care of yourself." He looked up from delving through the battered leather backpack, offered her a quick smile, then turned back to his search.

"I don't think so," she said slowly, mulling it over while trying not to look at him. He hadn't shaved this morning, as though he'd been in too much of a hurry or too distracted to be bothered. The dark overnight growth enhanced rather than obscured his features. After the days of increasing intimacy, it was unsettling to see him like this, with so many of society's little disguises removed. She shifted, drawing her isolation around her like a protective cloak. "No, I think you have some latent nurturing tendencies. You seem to need to take care of those who are weaker."

⌘⌘

Her analysis stopped him cold. Setting the backpack down, he rested his forearm on one upraised knee and regarded her closely. There was a new, defensive note in her quietly cultured voice and signs of even thicker walls than before.

She'd been sitting on the rock, looking out over the valley, watching her fool of a dog pretend to hunt. So alone. A notebook lay open on her knee but he doubted much had been written.

No, she'd been brooding, trying to reconcile a few days of emotion and caring against an eternity of desolation. In any equation, the balance would be all wrong. Since she thought she'd learned long before that no one could possibly want to care for her, she had to dredge up some reason for his concern. Her solution made him madder than hell.

"You're wrong." He said managed to keep his voice level as he reached for a towel-wrapped bundle. The towel opened out into a respectable boulder cloth, revealing breakfast sandwiches of bagels and thick sliced ham. "Not quite the arches, but I prefer the decor." He pulled out a cup for himself, filled it with coffee, covered the thermos and put it to one side. "Come and eat, Bethany."

"Don't you ever listen to me? I was just inexcusably rude." Drawing her heavy over-shirt closed around herself, she shifted until she faced him, legs tucked under her body. She sipped at the coffee, ignoring the sandwich.

"If you were inexcusably rude, it's just as well I don't listen to you, isn't it? Eat your breakfast before your idiot child steals it."

He figured she had to admit this was an understandable request, especially since she could see Baron coming around a tree, bearing down on them at a ragged gallop. The burst of energy lasted him only long enough to collapse at her feet, panting heavily.

Before Bethany could offer her sandwich, Jonathan reached into the backpack, coming up with a handful of dog biscuits. Deterred from this solution to meal disposal, she picked up the fragrant sandwich, wrapped the bottom half in a napkin and bit into it.

When she remembered to eat, Bethany enjoyed her food more whole-heartedly than any woman he'd ever known. Her eyes half-closed in appreciation, she took dainty bites, chewing slowly and letting the goodness make its way through her body. It was amazingly erotic and made him think of being appreciated one slow bite at a time. At least she hadn't bundled up. The morning was too brisk for bare arms, but she hadn't buttoned the large rust-brown shirt worn over a loose tan-colored cotton shell.

"You working in the open air?" He indicated her notebook while refilling both coffee cups.

"Not really." Finishing her sandwich, she rolled the napkin into a tight ball and pushed it into the backpack. "I was mostly gathering impressions and trying to shake off the after effects of a video marathon." She raised one leg, and rested her chin on her upraised knee, again contemplating the sky and the valley below them.

As he had done so often lately, Jonathan ignored the familiar beauty of his land to study this perplexing, fascinating intrusion on his privacy. Her hair lay gracefully on her shoulders. Her eyes, deep pools of mystery, blinked sleepily at him until she dredged up the brief animosity. Then they sparked with her extreme intelligence and strong will.

"What do you think of drive-in movies?" he asked, wanting her to direct some of that intelligence his direction.

"As an art form, they rank somewhat below amateur theater and above home videos." She managed to inject a perfect tone of hauteur, but a smile quivered at the corners of her mouth.

"And as a form of social interaction?"

She shrugged, still not quite meeting his gaze. There was a stillness to her he hadn't sensed before, a settling of the inner turmoil that made him hope she was finding peace with her life, and his part in it. He hoped the healing would continue through all the revelations.

"Bethany?" He spoke softly, his voice a part of the breeze. She turned her head slightly toward where he lounged, meeting his eyes with the shyness of a newly tamed foal. "Honey, why don't you ever touch me?"

As a question it ranked right up there with the Spanish Inquisition for shock value. Any semblance of peace vanished as she pulled herself rigidly upright. She didn't physically jump up and flee, but every angle of her body leaned away from him.

"What an utterly ridiculous question." Her response brought icy hauteur to a new level. "I have touched you."

"Let me count the times," he misquoted, attempting to defuse some of the tension. "It would be easy, there have been damned few."

"But—well—" she floundered, gulping air. "I don't touch." The explanation brought her instant relief, and she was able to relax somewhat, releasing the intense quivering of her muscles.

"Bull."

"It's nothing personal, Jonathan," she hastened to explain. "I'm just not a touching sort of person. I never have been."

"I've seen you touch. Plenty of times."

"When—where?" Spluttering indignation rid her of the last vestiges of tension.

"You touch Baron all the time."

The near smile hovered, threatening to form a real dimple beside her mouth. An obviously unaccustomed sense of the ridiculous lit up her eyes and she even managed a tiny nose wrinkle.

"Baron is a dog," she explained as though to a sweet but simple child.

"Baron is the most important creature in your life. I'm only asking to be treated like you treat your dog." He managed to remain absolutely still, leaning back on his hands, in spite of the worry he felt over pushing her like this. But time was running out, in so many ways. "How do you pet Baron, Bethany?"

She stared at her hands, clenched together tightly in her lap. It was so little he was asking, or was it? Just an expression of trust among friends. Just a slight lowering of a few minor barriers. Just everything.

253

"Sometimes," she said very softly, "I rub his ears, and scratch along the top of his head."

Had she been looking up, she would have seen Jonathan's eyes closing briefly then a grin flashing across his face. What she saw instead was a head of thick, dark hair, placed within easy reach. His hands were jammed firmly into the pockets of his jacket.

Her fingers touched in the shyest fashion. She fluttered strokes along his scalp and briefly around his suddenly ultra-sensitive ear, activating nerve endings he was sure were unknown to modern science. Then the exquisite fingers lifted, curling into her palms and moving back to rest in her lap.

"Surely you can do better than that." He spoke through lips held taut with frustration. "If that was all you ever did for Baron, he would've chosen to stay with Paul years ago."

"I don't underst—"

"I've watched stroke that dog until he melted into a puddle of sensation. You can spare me more than a few timid touches."

As if emboldened by his taunting words, Bethany once more lifted her hands. This time she framed his face between her palms, starting at his cheeks and stroking downward until her fingers covered his jaw. Leaning forward slightly, she shifted her hold, plunging her fingers once again into his hair, covering his ears with her palms. The tips of her fingers tensed and relaxed, rotating against his scalp while his ear was gently, thoroughly, enticingly massaged. Her body relaxed forward, her forehead coming within heat distance of his.

Jonathan felt her ease forward, her resistance lessening as she became more involved. Even as he savored the closeness, he felt his body crying out for more. He knew there could be so much more, if she could only put the past behind her and let this grow between them.

"I've seen you hug him from time to time," he murmured, daring her to continue. It was a calculated risk that paid off as she leaned even further forward, letting her hands rest on his back. Her body warmth reached out to him from brow to waist. "And rub your cheek along his—"

As though mesmerized, Bethany allowed herself to close the distance, touching her soft cheek along the harshness of his. After a heartbeat of hesitation, she eased forward, resting her weight against his chest. His hands remained pocketed, but his muscles stiffened. It would be difficult to say whose heart beat harder.

"And sometimes, you let him rub you back." Not daring to shift his weight enough to bring her against him as he wanted to, Jonathan allowed himself only the liberty to slide his face gently along hers. The scent of her, the thought of the soft skin at the base of her neck, drew him like a magnet. Breathing deeply, he buried his face in the richness of her hair until he was nuzzling her neck. His mouth opened, tongue daring to dart out, to taste her skin and know her at least in this small way.

അയ

It was suddenly too much. Straightening her arms, she pushed against him. Her fingers seemed reluctant to leave his leanly muscled back but they finally obeyed. There was a moment of mutiny, when her hands begged to be allowed to at least rest on his shoulders, enjoying the strength and promised safety there. Trembling, she pulled away from him, rising to her knees and then to her feet, putting distance between them. In an attempt to forestall any anger on his part, she began to button her over shirt, looking around for her notebook.

"I need to get back to work on the interview while my notes are fresh. I should have it done by—" she was babbling, and even that faded as Jonathan surged to his feet. His height became more imposing when he took a firm step toward her. "Now what do you want?"

His reply was audible but non-verbal as he closed the distance between them. He stopped just inside her limit of personal space. He still didn't speak but his attitude was one of anger and—disappointment?

"You told me you wanted me to touch you the way I touch my dog," she challenged. "I did what you wanted. I touched you."

"I lied." Frustration and impatience roughened his voice. "I want you to touch me the way you touch a man. You were married. You know how."

"Virgin brides don't touch their husbands," she said, allowing the painful memo-

257

ries of helplessness to show in her voice and actions.

"You're not a virgin bride. And I'm not your husband." Before she could escape this time for good, his large, warm, hands descended on her shoulders. "Bethany, you are a magnificently sexy woman." He spoke slowly, his eyes daring her to believe him, to believe in herself. "And I'm a man who's going to explode if you don't touch me properly."

ოოო

She'd gone icy pale and that blank lost look had come back into her eyes. For a moment he was bitterly afraid his impatience had pushed her away, when all he wanted was to bring her ever closer. Then she drew a deep breath, and delicate color flowed back into her face. An irrepressible dimple snuck onto her cheek as though it had always lived there.

"We can't have that," she murmured in a low, husky tone he'd never heard before. "Who would clean up the mess?"

Her hands rose again, resting on his shoulders as his hands dropped to hang at his sides.

There was a further moment of indecision, when her eyes asked for, then found, reassurance in the taut lines of his face.

"Go ahead, Bethany," he urged, striving to keep his voice evenly pitched, to not grab her while she hesitated, her eyes enormous as she studied his face. "You can touch me any way you want."

The delicate hands lifted, trembling slightly, to stroke along his unshaven jaw, trail down his neck, touch briefly on his pulse, cup strong shoulders under his soft shirt. Jonathan held himself absolutely still, fearing any carelessness on his part would destroy her courage. Slender fingers slid down his arms, hesitating at the rolled-up sleeves before venturing onto the haired surface of his forearms.

Bethany curved her hands until her palms lightly cupped his arms, pleasuring herself with the sensations. When she reached his hands she traced to the ends of his fingers, then slowly felt between his fingers until their hands were linked, hers covering his. She hesitated, as if relishing the touch of the inner edges of their fingers along their entire length.

Jonathan shook from the need for restraint. When her eyes drifted half shut and her mouth parted, breath deepening into intense sensual enjoyment, he almost lost it. Moving slowly, he slid his fingers along the length of her palm, then covered her hands with his own, cupping her fingers warmly. Her eyes widened fractionally when he guided her hands to his waist, then down. She tried to resist, but let him place her hands in intimate contact with his body. Even through the sturdy denim he knew she could feel his heat and the anticipatory heavy strength of him. When he stirred, hardening even more under her touch, she attempted to pull her hands away.

"Not to worry, precious," he said, his voice strained. "That's just me, wanting you."

He replaced her hands, increasing the pressure until she cupped him, stroking along his waiting length. Her touch became progressively bolder while he held her hips, his fingers digging in slightly. His sweating forehead rested against hers as he battled the urge to take her right then, and damn the consequences. Muttering a hoarse curse, he grabbed her wrists, allowing himself the brief luxury of flexing against her while he trembled even more, then gently pulled her hands away from his body.

Jonathan straightened, grimacing, and his eyes squeezed shut. When his eyes opened, he met her wondering green gaze and smiled ruefully, taking in her softened expression with an unholy surge of joy. He leaned back, looking down at their linked hands, then at her. He smiled, almost gently.

Slowly, he raised her hands, touching her fingers to his lips, moistening her fingertips. His tongue ventured briefly between her fingers, before he guided her hands inexorably to touch her hardening nipples. He pressed her fingertips against her body in a delicate caress.

"And that's you, wanting me."

For a moment she tensed. Then she snatched her hands away from his hold, leaving his large palms cupping her breasts, thumbs stroking her straining nipples. Her fingers dug into the clenched muscles of his forearms and he tried to think of all the reasons he should pull his hands away. He could only think of warm breezes surging across a meadow, and overheated bodies inextricably entwined.

"J—Jonathan." Her voice was a tight whisper laced with fright and wanting.

He let his hands stray lower until he could cup the lush derriere that had fascinated him for days. It was even more wonderful than his most erotic fantasies. He held her, stroking her, urging her to move even closer, enjoying the sweet ache of his aroused flesh pressing into her softness—and her not pulling away.

"Jonathan?"

So much was in that hesitant voice—hope, fear, a question. Not relinquishing his hold, he felt the unbearable tension began to drain away. They rocked together, breath warming each other's necks, while sanity began to slowly reassert itself.

"Not yet. Soon, precious, but not yet."

His voice was harsher than ever. She had to feel him, hard and hurting, against her stomach.

"But—this isn't—I'm not being nice to you."

He smiled, and flexed his body against hers, lifting her up until they meshed perfect-ly. "This is very nice. It will be even nicer when you're really ready." His hold shifted, and he let her feet return to the ground. He held her more loosely now but still touched as much of her as he could until the need lessened and they could breathe normally.

"Jonathan?" she whispered again, hesitantly, as if not daring to lift her head and meet his eyes. "What are we doing?"

Jonathan wondered when he'd laughed last. He'd wanted to see a real smile on Bethany's face, but had never thought about how long it'd been for him. Burrowing his face under her hair, he gave himself up to the healing laughter.

"That seems pretty obvious to me, precious," he managed to gasp between chuckles.

Expelling a breath that managed to express her disgust at his display, Bethany pushed back against his hold. Her forearms braced against his chest, she tilted her head, looking up into his face. He was making a serious effort to control his mirth, but there was no way he could hide the underlying expression on his face. He must have looked—happy.

"Not this," she began, a small frown pulling her brows together as she searched for words. "Well, not precisely. What are you doing, and why are you doing it?"

Those tiny lines between her brows made her look like a worried pixie. The sensuous haze had left her remarkable eyes but there was a new richness and depth to them, and soft strength to her mouth that had not been there before. He ached to feel her lips against his in a kiss without end. But those lips were parting and the words that came out were serious.

"Why are we doing this?"

He loosened his hold, letting her weight rest against the circle of his arms. In spite of her worry, she still trusted him enough to remain close. It was a special sort of trust.

"We're becoming friends. Good friends. Special friends."

She'd never had a special friend. Not really, and her face showed it. That the possibility interested her also showed.

"You need a friend, and out of all the people I've ever known, you deserve one." He pulled her close again, in a comforting rather than passionate embrace. His cheek nuzzled into the fragrant softness of her hair and his hands soothed along her back. He stared, unseeing, at the growing beauty of the day. "You deserve so much."

"Are you offering yourself for this position?" She'd managed to keep her tone light, though he could tell she felt once again as though they were talking at cross purposes.

"If you'll have me." When she would have questioned his bleak statement, he released her, reaching down for the backpack. "Let's get back to the house. I'll explain there."

CHAPTER 12

Once they were back at the house, Bethany followed Jonathan to his studio. Settling her in a large chair near the window, he found a pillow to stuff behind her back and a stool for her to prop up her feet.

"Some coffee? Maybe sandwiches and milk or iced tea?"

"Jonathan," she warned softly. "You're nurturing again." Her voice was amused but she couldn't hide the subdued anxiety behind her words. In spite of three years of marriage, she was ignorant of so much of what went on between a man and a woman. She felt shaken, her heart racing far more than the simple walk back to the house could justify.

Jonathan reached inside a cupboard, bringing out an old cardboard box.

"It's past time to get all the skeletons out of the closet," he said quietly. "I found this a couple evenings ago." He held the box between his hands, staring at the lid as though he could see inside. "You wanted to see some of my early work. Mom has what I did before I left for Europe, but the rest of it's right here." He set the box in her lap, pausing for a moment before removing the lid. "You can look at anything in here that interest you. I'm going to get us some lunch. If you have any questions, I'll answer them when I get back. Any questions at all."

Bethany watched him leave, troubled by his actions. She could remember Jonathan being agitated when he'd helped her down from the tree. Every other occasion, he was able to draw from some inner well of control, as though he had learned to be apart from normal upsets and worries.

She looked at the box in her lap, and felt the pull of all the individuals who made up her character. Her ability to wall off the different segments of her personality had gotten her through the travesty of her marriage. Now BL Acton, reporter extraordinaire, was itching to go through the treasure that had been dropped in her lap. Lulu was deathly afraid of the box. In there could very well be something that would destroy what little she and Jonathan had managed to create. Bethany, the newest of her emerging personalities, wanted to set the box aside and go comfort Jonathan.

For long minutes she ran her fingers along the upper edges of the photographs, lightly touching the dividers. Each had a title, scrawled in Jonathan's distinctive illegible handwriting. There was potential hurt and fear because of that, in this box. Here was a past neither one of them seemed to want to remember, but could not forget. There might also be a key here to their future, and she refused to allow the past to ruin that. She pulled out the first group of photos.

The work was distinctively J. Phillip Merritt. Whether of children playing around a pond, old women gossiping in the market or farmers patiently turning their fields behind plows pulled by stolid draft horses, the photos shared a mastery of balance and illumination. Even then, he had possessed an instinctive knowledge of the perfect moment when pressing the shutter would create an image of soul-wrenching beauty. These prints represented the best culled from a large number of shots taken. But she knew from her own bitter, near laughable experience that quantity of photos had no bearing on quality.

She studied each image, for the first time not averse to remembering what it had been like to grow up in Europe. She could almost smell the air in the markets and on the shores, and memories became clearer and sweeter.

At first, when she started to go through the group of photos at the back of the box, she was unaware of how the subject matter had changed. From simple country scenes and intricately lighted still lifes, she came upon rather mundane shots of girls at play. The artistic ability was still obvious. The photos were exhilarating images of flying hair, fresh complexions, bright eyes and long legs.

She quickly identified girls in a private school, at some sort of athletic competition. They all wore uniforms which allowed for maximum mobility and exposed discreet amounts of skin. Then the settings and uniforms became personally familiar. Putting the box to one side, she concentrated on the photos in her hands.

"Omigod, that's Melly! Kate—Bonnie—Steph. Where did he get these?" She spoke under her breath in a kind of awed bemusement. It was obvious Jonathan had taken a sequence of girls at exercise. But why?

She could even remember the day and the event. It had been a parent's day, and there'd been a soccer match. She could almost hear the laughter and feel the excitement. She'd been captain of the winning team. Then she came to a set of photos of an enchanting, long-legged, laughing girl, holding up the ball in victory. The girl was grinning into the camera, tossing her auburn ponytail over her shoulder as she dodged a bucket of water flung by her teammates. Bethany felt every tendon in her body contract.

"But this is—how old was I?"

"Somewhere around fourteen, as close as I can figure."

Jonathan came into the room with an air of studied nonchalance but she knew him too well now to be fooled by his sophisticated veneer. He set a laden tray on a low table, and then sat down in a corner of the couch, twisting so he could look directly in her eyes. It was obvious he wanted to look anywhere but in her eyes. Bethany refused a sandwich but accepted a cup of coffee while she waited for him to start explaining.

"I'd been free lancing for a couple of years, weddings, parties, society functions. Occasionally I sold some of my informal pieces. Then Marlene told me about someone who needed photo illustrations for a series of articles on girl's schools for a prestigious international magazine. It would have been a big step up in my career." He spoke slowly, weighing every word as it was chosen, as if saying this right was critical. "We ended up going to five or six schools and shooting up rolls of film.

"I used slide film, of course, and only printed the better shots. Marlene told me the article was rejected, but never explained why. I was paid generously for my efforts, and that seemed to be the end of it. Except I had made duplicates of a few of the shots, because of these." He reached for the photos she held loosely in her hands, and sorted through them. As he came to the ones he was searching for, he displayed them. "You were so happy that day, so lovely. You had the world at your feet and your whole wonderful life ahead of you. When I look back now, that day was one of the brightest spots in that period of my life."

For the first time, Jonathan looked away, reaching to refill his coffee cup from the carafe on the tray. He stared at the oversized photo of the yacht on the wall, and then continued, his words coming with an obvious effort.

"Your wedding, two years later, was the darkest. That was when I discovered the article had been a farce. Stefan Dubec wanted to pick out his future bride, and the arrogant, ignorant American was stupid enough to be happy to take the pictures."

"That was the day everything changed," she murmured, her voice as remote as her eyes had once been. "A week after the parent's day, I was transferred to that new school I told you about before. Very exclusive, very strict, very expensive. I asked Papa how he could afford it. He told me he had made some investments to ensure my future.

"After that, there were no more games, no more holidays at the homes of the other girls. I was given extra lessons and special treatment by the staff. I was also guarded more strictly than anyone else in the school. I couldn't even speak with the seventy-year old gardener!" Her fingers spasmed, and she came perilously near spilling her coffee. "If I had known then that I was being prepared as a virgin sacrifice, I would have stripped myself naked and thrown myself on a table in a waterfront bar!"

◊◊◊

Jonathan took away her cup and dared to hold her cold hands between his. When she didn't pull away immediately, he squeezed gently, turning her until their knees met.

"I would like to think if I had known I would have tried to do something to help you. But I was such a consummate bastard then. I wanted to be something more than Johnnie Merritt who had been the president of the high school photo club. As it ended up, I was far less."

Her hands twisted in his, seeking to mesh with his fingers and offer comfort. Any remnant of betrayal she may have felt upon realizing how completely his talent with a camera had affected her life seemed to be overcome by his absolute candor.

"Are you carrying a load of guilt about this? How could you have known? It was the

Twentieth Century, not Medieval Europe. Who could—"

"I knew what kind of depraved slime they were," he interrupted ruthlessly. "But I refused to admit I'd become one of them. I played their games and took their pictures and pretended I was better than they were."

"But you—"

"After your wedding," he continued in the same ruthlessly toneless voice, "I took these pictures to my wife and asked her if what I heard while I was taking wedding pictures was true, that I had set you up for this marriage. Marlene laughed at me. She laughed at me a lot, and I hadn't really noticed before. She said it was cute that I had kept pictures of all the pretty little girls and offered to arrange something with you, once Stefan got tired of his virgin bride. She thought it wouldn't take long." His disgust was as real now as it had been then—at his wife for the offer and at himself for being tempted to take her up on it.

Bethany paled as he spoke and pulled her hands back to clench them in her lap.

"That was one indignity I never suffered. Stefan was too possessive, too arrogant. He liked to flaunt his treasures in front of everyone, letting them know that what he had, no one else could touch. His guards, and their dogs, were well paid to ensure the sanctity of Stefan's possessions. No one but his staff was allowed to touch me. Nor could I touch them."

Jonathan looked at the laughing girl in the photos, hugging her friends, kissing her father on the cheek, linking arms with one of the teachers. Touching, always touching, giving of her warmth and love to everyone around her.

"Every morning, my hair was washed and styled, my face was made up and I was given something white to wear. Usually a bikini. I was kept lightly tanned, to better show off the white."

Understanding came upon him like a bolt of lightning.

"That's why all the disguises? The baggy dark rags from chin to toe?"

"I suppose so," she admitted. "It was never a conscious decision. I don't think I could ever wear white again. Even pastels make me nauseous."

Jonathan lifted a hand to lay it gently on her hair. He wasn't sure what else he could do. With a background like hers had been, it was a miracle she'd allowed him to come as close as he had.

"My hair—Stefan was enamored of a certain French actress-dancer. He wanted my hair short and dark, and I had to exercise constantly. He hated my butt." The crudity seemed to come without any effort. It was obvious she'd heard the term so often it had lost any potential to shock.

"More fool he. Your 'butt,' your derriere, your tush, has been driving me crazy from the first day I saw you." He waited for the words to sink through her layers of fear and insecurity. When she raised large, bright eyes to his, he nodded, smiling slightly. "But we'll discuss that later."

Sliding his hand reluctantly from the softness of her hair, he refilled their coffee cups and handed hers back to her.

"Your wedding was the last time I photographed people," he began again, wanting to get it all out so that they could get on with the business of life. "I asked about Stefan Dubec's wife before I left Europe. I was told she died."

"I got pregnant, about a year after we were married," she said quietly. "Stefan was furious

276

at first. But I'd only gone to strict Catholic schools. I didn't even know the word contraception. He decided having his young wife pregnant made him look good and he began to plan a wardrobe that would emphasize his potency. I was naive enough to think this meant he was happy with me as his wife. A few days later, I found him in bed with two of his favorites and I stupidly tried to leave the yacht. I slipped on the dock and miscarried; I was ill for a long time."

Jonathan nodded his understanding, afraid to speak. The extent of her suffering was too great for him to even pretend to imagine. He offered his hand, silently, in a long overdue attempt to comfort. After a moment, she took it between both of hers, and hung on.

"Stefan was furious. I'd lost the proof of his virility, and I wasn't even pretty any more. Papa came back sometime around then." She looked in turn at the magnificent, malevolent ship. "He was appalled, and furious with himself. They wouldn't let him visit too often. He told me to get well and stay ready and gave me the name of his lawyer. When The Lulu—blew up," she swallowed, closing her eyes against the tears. "We were in harbor with her. I was able to get away in the confusion. He must have planned it that way.

"Papa's lawyer hid me, got me to this country, made sure I had whatever I needed. Somehow, he managed a divorce, and I took my mother's maiden name. I took nothing from my marriage." She paused, gaining control as the memories lost their stranglehold. "I never heard from Stefan again. I guess he decided to write me off as a bad investment."

Her fingers were unconsciously seeking comfort by rubbing around and through his fingers and palm. In spite of the gravity of their discussion, it was getting harder and harder to not let her touch affect him. It was as though, by revealing the truth of her past to him, she was allowing herself to put it behind her and was trying to reach out to him. He hoped desperately he wasn't misreading the situation.

"I didn't know what Stefan did or did not do, and I've been afraid of upsetting you by accidentally doing something he did." He searched her face for reaction as he spoke. It might have been a risky time to try to probe at her but she seemed more open with him now than she had ever been.

"Is that why you keep acting the way you do?"

"How do I act?" His confusion was obvious.

"You keep getting me all excited, then you back off," she said grumpily, looking astonished at her daring.

His bark of laughter was as welcome as it was unexpected by both of them. Cradling her chin between his palms, he allowed the warmth of his smile to spread across his whole face.

"Yes, you little nuisance, that was why."

"Oh." She turned away, adroitly removing her face from his grasp. The coffee cup was empty again, and she set it down.

He felt his agitation increasing, but waited for some kind of a sign from her. Something to tell him she didn't equate his presence with the depravity of being Stefan's wife. "Kissing," she said softly.

"I beg your pardon?" He could not have been more surprised if she had thrown herself on him naked, nor more pleased. She was speaking in an undertone and fiddling with the cuff of her appallingly ugly flannel shirt, but she had said...

"Kissing." It was no louder this time.

"I understand that much. Kissing is a good thing."

"Stefan was never very fond of kissing." If possible, her voice was even softer. A deep rose color began to rise up her neck.

The blush was delightful. He couldn't remember ever seeing such a charming blush. He wanted to track that blush to its source.

"Are you trying to tell me something, Bethany?" He could afford to tease her now that some kind of an end was in sight. He wondered what she would say next, and prompted her ruthlessly. "If you want to tell me something, just be direct. I won't take it the wrong way."

"Would—you—please—kiss—me— Jonathan!" she ground out between suddenly clenched teeth.

"I thought you'd never ask."

Their eyes remained opened, forest glades staring into the blue of a high-country summer sky. Then her face came too close to see more than the length of her lashes as his eyes closed, and she slowly lowered her own lids.

Their breaths mingled, warm and smelling of coffee as his smile settled against her lips.

Her mouth was soft and trembling slightly, reminding him in this area she definitely lacked experience. Still, he'd hoped for more from their first kiss than patient acceptance. Perhaps not a full frontal tongue assault, and definitely having her on a set of pale turquoise sheets was out of the picture for the moment, though the image was certainly appealing enough. But something to show that she was participating. Then he felt her sigh enter his mouth, gliding over the tongue that had been probing, ever so gently, against her lips.

Steady, he warned himself. You may be ready for a duel of the tongues but if you blow this invitation it could be a cold day in Hades before you get another one. Even as he was giving his tongue severe orders it was sliding through her parted lips, hunting, seeking its perfect mate. Along the way, he sampled the heat of her inner lip, the smooth serration of her teeth, the warm sweetness of her mouth.

Bethany's hands shook against his chest as she edged a hair closer, making the joining even more seamless. For the longest time, an eternity at least, if not a full minute, his lips warmed hers. Then he tore his mouth away, holding himself at sufficient distance to avoid ravaging her on the spot. Bethany was definitely not an educated kisser, but she was learning at a speed equivalent to a Mensa rating. Her lashes lifted, and the invitation in her eyes was delightfully clear. He swooped forward, stealing a quick taste from her and escaping before she could respond.

"Could—" She cleared her throat. "Could we do that again, please?"

He felt his smile spread throughout his body. She sounded like she was in an advanced deportment class. Kissing 201. The idea had possibilities. Particularly if he could choose the student body. It would be even better if he could touch the student body. He swooped again, gliding his tongue into her mouth, exploring briefly, then retreating. This time, he dropped a kiss on her nose for good measure.

"Jon—a—than!"

Before she could pull her tongue back from forming his name, he assaulted it again.

"Do you want me to stop?" He spoke between quick, biting, licking, kisses scattered around her mouth, touching everywhere but her lips.

"*No!*"

She was rewarded by a kiss lasting perhaps a full five seconds.

"If you want me to slow down, you'll have to slow me down."

Uttering a brief huff of exasperation, Bethany took hold of his face between her hands, quickly sliding them until her fingers nested in the thickness of his hair and her palms could caress his ears.

When he felt her long slender fingers plunge into his hair, holding him an eager and willing captive, Jonathan wanted to yell in triumph. He didn't dare break the light-hearted sensual mood. Nor did he want her to think she wasn't in total control. The illusion of control had given her the courage to touch him, to hold him closer, and lean against him in a singular display of trust. Gently, slowly, he enfolded her in his arms.

When he shifted, when his hands left the back of the couch to cradle her body, alert for any sign of discomfort, she opened her mouth wider, tilting her head, inviting his invasion, and meeting it with a touch, tease, and glide maneuver he had shown her just a moment before. The effect was awesome. It was hard to tell which one of them shook more.

Jonathan found the sense to lean back, to pull away from the dangerous contact before he lost all control.

"Just give me a minute to breathe, precious," he managed in a hoarse voice.

"I never knew it was like that." Apparently, she couldn't manage much more than a croak herself. "Kissing, I mean."

He wanted to tell her that it wasn't, that only once in a very rare while was kissing anything like what they had just shared. He held his peace, and held her face against his neck, carefully keeping her from full body contact.

Jonathan knew he was a selfish bastard as a lover. Even in high school, he'd made it a point to choose partners capable of finding their own satisfaction and needing no guidance. He preferred to satisfy himself and leave. The small pleasures, holding hands, just being with a woman, touching her without it leading to sexual satisfaction, had never held any appeal for him.

He found himself enjoying just looking at Bethany sitting across a table from him, and he found uncommon pleasure in the increasing trust of her responses. Now she was cradled in his arms, melting against him after only a few, essentially chaste, kisses. He was trembling like a farm boy on his first date.

He shifted, resting his cheek against the wild tumble of her hair. Slowly, slowly, the trembling eased within her and the sharp edge of need drained away from both of them.

"You're going to do it again, aren't you?" Her small voice came from the juncture of his neck and shoulder and her breath was scorching him. He cradled her closer.

"Do what, precious?"

"You're going to get me all worked up and drop me again."

He had to laugh, a delighted chuckle that came from somewhere in his distant happy past and gained in strength. He rocked her against his body, torturing himself with the feel of her soft breasts against his chest.

"What makes you think I'm going to drop you?"

"The way you're acting, like you want me to pretend nothing happened and we're just buddies."

"Maybe I'm indulging in a few fantasies. And we are buddies. We're best buddies."

"You have fantasies?"

"Of course I have fantasies."

"What are your fantasies?" she asked, sounding wistful.

He thought of pastel sheets, family photo albums, an uninterrupted backdrop and hours, days, of time with no intrusions.

"You are, Bethany. You're my fantasy."

She went very still in his arms, and her head raised slowly. There were lines between her brows and a myriad of questions in her eyes. Shadows appeared and grew but did not fully take over her remarkably clear gaze. It was too soon to push her, he sensed, after their cathartic of emotion. Time to lighten the mood, seal it off with some laughter.

"Would you like to help me indulge in a specific fantasy?"

As he had thought she would, she became immediately, delightfully suspicious. Her head reared back, and she straightened her arms abruptly. Letting her go, he set his hands gently on her shoulders.

"It's a simple fantasy. Just you, me, dress-up clothes and dinner at a fancy restaurant. A date."

"Where would we go?" She wasn't sure she was ready for people.

"We could stay right here and play pretend again. We did well enough with the drive-in." He wasn't about to share her just yet. Time enough for that when they had to go back to civilization. By then there would be more trust between them. He hoped.

"I'm done with the framework of your interview, and most of the background color. It just needs a final write." It sounded like a non sequitur, but she must be trying to warn him how limited their time frame was. Perhaps she even wanted him to know there was no reason to continue to cater to her strangeness. "You still want to do this dress up thing?"

"More than ever. With that damned article out of the way, you'll have time to concentrate on learning how to have fun." He stared at her intensely, studying the changes, reveling in them, wishing they could be accelerated. "Come on, buddy. Go for it."

"So," she said on an obvious rush of courage. "What time is our reservation?"

CHAPTER 13

Bethany stared at herself in the steam fogged mirror. In the slash of clarity created by the swipe of a towel, she was attempting to pin up her hair. She hadn't realized how much mass it would attain when blown dry. A looser knot than normal made for a softer look, but she wondered how it would look properly styled. As she worked, she noticed the rough condition of her hands, the nails clean but functionally short. For so many years, her life had allowed for nothing else. She'd preferred it that way.

You are my fantasy. The words drifted insidiously through her head. What had he really meant?

She had to wonder if he referred to his long-time fascination with the photos of a young girl who had ceased to exist so many years before. Did he ever wish he had taken his wife up on her offer? Nothing was so potent as wondering what might have been.

If that were the case, if he wanted to indulge in a long buried fascination, could she refuse him? Jonathan had helped her lay to rest so many ghosts. Could she deny him anything, when his fantasies were so close to her own?

She couldn't believe he meant anything beyond an indulgence in impulses once rejected. No man of Jonathan's experience and status could be interested for long in an emotionally damaged neurotic of questionable background.

She stared solemnly at the green-eyed woman in the mirror while arranging the emerald silk gift which Marsha had included in the clothes sent. The colors brought out highlights in her hair and eyes she'd never before seen. An early lifetime of drab school uniforms, then the farce of only white clothing, had not prepared her for what rich jewel tones would look like against her skin.

An innate sense of style approved of the color and the material but was appalled at how the silk fit over her standard undergarments. The darker color was appropriate, but the heavy construction of her sturdy bra and cotton panties stood out markedly. This would never do.

"Bethany?" A soft knock accompanied Jonathan's voice. "Hurry up, honey, they won't hold our reservation forever."

The face in the mirror lost all pretense of solemnity. A smile began to form and she looked in wonder at the difference it made on her mouth. What would it be like if she and Jonathan were actually going out for dinner in reality? She knew she would take the memories offered by this nebulous fantasy time with him over the guarantee of security with anyone else.

"Why don't you go ahead and order?" she called out, keeping in the mood of the moment. "I'll be out in a few minutes."

❧❧

The table was set with fine dishes, illuminated by candles in silver holders. The wine was chilled. A simple meal stayed warm in chafing dishes. On the screen, the video was of spectacular canyons and rushing streams, set to a background of classical music. In the corner near the flickering fire, Baron had settled into his bed of quilts and pillows, sleeping after his evening meal and run.

The stage was set. The leading lady was due on at any minute. The leading man was nervous as hell. Tonight, he had to reach through Bethany's many—and justified—barriers to the woman whose growth had been suppressed ten years before. He had to do this before his own frustrated impulses took over his actions.

With no warning, she appeared in the entryway from the hall. Against the darkness, her skin had a luminous tone, enhanced by the deep green of loose, floating silk that clung lovingly in some places, flowed elegantly in others. It was either a dress of delightfully simple lines, full and feminine, slacks with a blouse. Whichever, an enchanting expanse of her pale chest was exposed by the bodice crossing over her breasts, fastened at her waistline by silver buttons.

Her hair was unusually abundant, pinned up loosely on her head, the length of neck exposed adding to the charm of her appearance. Uncommonly brilliant eyes peered at him warily and that delightful mischievous lower lip was starting to slide back between her teeth. She was a vision, and she looked to be at least as scared as he was.

Moving forward slowly, Jonathan extended his hand.

"Won't you come into my parlor?"

Bethany laid her fingers hesitantly on his warm palm. There was a strange glow in her eyes tonight, a welcoming tilt to her lips he'd never seen before. "Said the spider to the fly?" she joked, with a quaver in her voice.

"That's seems rather apt," he mused. "You are definitely a covered dish, and I'm beginning to feel more and more like a starving man."

Feeling the chill in the fingers nestled so trustingly in his, Jonathan reached for her other hand, and led her slowly into the room. The silk swirled around her, a river of deep green enhancing the curves of her body. It embraced her from shoulders to ankles, and eddied around her slender feet.

"Where are your shoes, Bethany?" His voice was warm and faintly amused.

"My things—" She cleared her throat, not quite meeting his eyes. "My things were too heavy to wear with this."

The blush rose again, spreading across the expanse of bared skin and up her graceful neck. Still holding her hands, Jonathan stepped backward, leading her off the chilly wood floor and onto the relative warmth of the thick wool rug by the fire. There he turned her slightly, positioning her so the warmth of the fire would reach her first. Then he understood the true meaning of the blush.

Not only her shoes had been too heavy for the elegance of her outfit. Backlit by the fire, the silk might as well have been transparent. And there was nothing else between her body and his sanity. Closing his eyes, Jonathan drew a deep breath, slid his hands up her shoulders, and turned her, shading her from the revealing glow of the fire.

"My compliments to your dressmaker, Miss Acton," he managed to say in a fairly normal tone of voice. "Is this a style you will be favoring often in the future?"

Her eyes fell and she began to play with one of the cast silver buttons holding the cuffs snugly together.

"M—Marsha found this for me. It's—I don't have fancy things. I never need them, and she's always trying to sneak something in when she does my laundry..." Her voice trailed away.

"I approve," Jonathan murmured, pulling her close for a chaste kiss on the forehead. "Most wholeheartedly, I do approve."

Setting her away from him, he began to gently knead her shoulders, willing her to look up. But the most he saw were dark red lashes, laying against the softness of her cheek. She was so nervous, so insecure about everything. It could have been no worse if she was totally inexperienced.

Then he reminded himself, in an angry aside, that total inexperience would have been far preferable to what Bethany knew of male-female relationships. The irony of the situation was that, except for a few teenage experiences, his knowledge of healthy associations was almost as lacking. It made for an interesting situation.

"Would you care to be seated? The menu this evening is simple but, I believe, quite tasty."

As he spoke he released her shoulders, taking her arm in an absolutely correct, formal fashion. A chair was already drawn out at the table, and he seated her with a flair, sliding the chair against her legs and sternly telling his eyes to stop looking down her front. He wondered if he could convince her to put a napkin around her neck, then decided he should be mature enough to sit across the table from her and not attack her. At least for a while.

☙❧

Bethany stared at the salad, seeing the torn greens and sliced tomatoes as a blur of stop and go. It was a delightful game Jonathan was playing with her, and he'd gone to so much trouble to make the setting as realistic as possible. He was dressed in finely woven dark slacks and shirt, fashionable yet comfortable and not overly formal. But she wasn't sure if she was up to a lot more play acting. She was restless, the blood racing through her body in an odd syncopated rhythm that somehow matched her occasional gasping breaths.

"I have a marvelous idea," she said, in the light voice she had once perfected to survive in a dangerous world. "As long as we're pretending, why don't we pretend we've already eaten? I don't think I'm very hungry."

Maybe it was an effect of the subdued lighting from the fire and the candles. It seemed as though Jonathan's face was softening and his eyes were melting into pools of blue warmth. Silly notion. Certainly he couldn't know how gauche and ill-prepared she was feeling. Neither her lessons in advanced deportment nor her associations with the financially elite had prepared her for intimate dinners with men whose lightest touch sent sparks flying through her body. He touched her now, a lingering stroke of one finger along the back of her hand.

"You've been pretending to eat most of the day. At the risk of being accused of nurturing, I must insist that you eat for real. Besides," he added, with a sudden, slashing grin, "you're going to need to keep up your strength."

❧❧

The video was now of forests in the springtime. A new log had been added to the fire and it was producing almost as much heat externally as the fine brandy produced internally. Curled in a corner of the couch, her feet tucked underneath herself, Bethany barely recognized these sources of heat. Nothing could equal the warmth of her thoughts.

Jonathan had kept the atmosphere during dinner very light, soothing any tensions she may have had. How could he know how deeply the insecurities were rooted? She had a feeling he did know. Somehow, she was going to have to find the courage to overcome her misgivings, or risk going no further in this relationship.

Throughout the meal she'd managed to maintain a veneer of worldly sophistication, relying on old methods to keep panic at bay. Surely, they would continue to work for her as they had in the past.

He came across the room toward her. Backlit by the fire, his face was in shadow, but there was subtle menace in the way he stalked toward her. Expecting him to use the other end of the couch, as he had been so carefully formal all evening, she jumped when he sat down next to her, nudging her feet with his lean-muscled thigh.

Instant heat came through the layers of cloth and warmed her chilled feet. But that was nothing compared to the warmth that flowed over her shoulders and along her side when he lifted an arm around her neck, pulling her against him.

"This is certainly cozy, isn't it?" he asked, stifling a yawn and stretching somewhat.

A nasty suspicion raced through her. "Is this where you tell me how tired you are and how restful I am? We've played out this scenario already, Mr. Merritt."

Soft laughter shook him, and he brought up his other hand to take hold of her shoulder, resting his arm lightly across her chest. "Not quite," he murmured, shifting until he could pull more of her weight against his waiting body. "This is where I tell you that I can't think of anywhere I'd rather be at this particular moment, except here, with you." He let the sincerity of his voice penetrate until she finally looked up. "Unless we could have less clothes and even closer contact."

There was no doubting his meaning. Bethany could picture them on the couch, firelight playing over their entwined bodies. The image was so sharp, so real, she jerked in a breath, nearly spilling her brandy.

"Careful there. Here, let me show you the very best way to drink brandy." His long-fingered hand stroked down her arm, cupping her fingers around the bulb of the snifter. Deftly, he lifted the brandy from her precarious grip. For a moment, he swirled the potent liquid in the oversized glass globe. When she would have looked away from his face and at the brandy, he cupped her cheek with his other hand, holding her in position. Without looking away from her dazed eyes, he lifted the glass to his mouth, tipping in the brandy with a quick flick of his wrist. Then he bent his head.

Jonathan was getting closer and closer, a smile barely lifting the corners of his mouth. The snifter ended up somewhere else and his hand settled on her throat, tilting her face just a little bit more. A gentle thumb pressed on her chin, and his mouth settled softly against her eager lips.

Heat exploded as the brandy transferred from his mouth to hers. Heat coursed through her veins, bubbled in her arteries, rioted in her stomach. Heat radiated from his hands cradling her face, his body alongside her, his chest pressing against her breasts. The heady fumes of the brandy filled their mouths and their minds, the fire between them that had been banked all evening flaring out of control.

With a desperate gasp, Jonathan wrenched him mouth away from the enticement of hers, his breathing labored. A soft whimper from deep in her throat almost sent him immediately back, but he knew if he kissed her again right now, he wouldn't stop. And she needed, she deserved, so much more. She was leaning against him, trusting him, clutching him, her weight fully against his chest. Her mouth was swollen, her eyes hazy with passion gone wild. He was still afraid to risk more.

Stalling, he looked up into her hair, as though noticing for the first time that it was pinned up. Attempting to lighten the mood, he went on a hairpin hunt, blithely tossing them away when found. When he was done, her glorious hair fell across her shoulders, down her back, around his hands.

"It lasted longer than I thought it would," Bethany noted, her voice far steadier than he had expected.

It felt so good, so very right, to have her resting against him like this. Still, he hesitated to take the next step, unwilling to push too far.

She lifted her head from its proper resting place on his shoulder.

"Jonathan, you're not planning to drop me again, are you?" she asked in a voice that sounded a bit breathless, a bit hopeful.

"Precious, if you fall this time, I'll be right there with you," he whispered, stroking along her back, reveling in the uninterrupted thrill of silk against silken skin. "I'll want to be underneath you when you land." He leaned closer, invitingly.

This time, *she* kissed *him*, a bit aggressively, biting softly at his mouth as she rose to her knees, entrusting her full weight to his care. He let her push him further back on the couch, deftly shifting as he fell back, until he was stretched out full length, and she was on top of him. She lifted her head, holding his face still between her hands, then shimmied, trying to move an inch closer to his mouth.

"Here, precious, just a hair closer—there," he slid his hands further down her back, cupping her derriere, lifting his knee to bring their bodies into more intimate contact.

❧❧❧

302

Bethany blinked. Jonathan's pupils had expanded to large black orbs, ringed by irises the smoky blue of a late evening in the desert. There was still a smile on his wide mouth, but it had a pained twist in the corners. She shifted experimentally, and felt his brandy enriched breath flow over her lips when he moaned.

"You want me," she marveled, feeling a leap further down his body to match the flare in his eyes.

"It's not something I can hide very easily, Bethany," he pointed out in a wry tone.

"No, you want *me*."

Comprehension dawned in those hypnotic, passion-darkened blue eyes. She felt his fingers flex, sinking luxuriously into her derriere, pulling her closer still. His hips lifted underneath hers, stroking then holding still for a long, trembling minute.

"I want *you*, Bethany," he said firmly. His hands swept up her body, nearly crushing her against his chest while his legs lifted and hugged her legs. "God, how I want you, need you."

Never had she heard such honest need in a man's voice. She doubted her husband had ever needed her as more than a plaything. She could not doubt Jonathan needed her. It was thrilling, exciting, and a bit frightening. She lifted against his hold, and he loosened the crushing hug immediately.

"So," she said a bit breathlessly. "Take me. What's stopping you this time?"

ℰⱯℰⱯ

"Brat," he breathed against her mouth before touching it in a quick stroking kiss. "I only want what you want to give me." His legs shifted, unwrapping from around hers. Then he slid a leg between hers, lifting against her in a soft vibration. "Such an expression. Bethany. Here, lift up."

His hands assisted her, tenderly urging, until she was sitting up, her knees hugging his lean hips. Her hands rested against his chest, elbows locked in a sudden surge of shyness at the new intimacy of their position. Jonathan stroked slowly along her tense forearms until she could adjust to the sensations. Then he felt warm, smooth skin instead of silk.

"What's this?"

"It's made in layers," she said tensely, arching her back as if in an excess of passion. "The slacks do that, also."

It was too obvious an invitation to pass up. Leaving her arms with reluctance, his fingers shifted to her knees and up her thighs. This time he found the openings immediately.

"We must ask where Marsha found this delightful outfit. I think your wardrobe needs some additional refurbishing." As he spoke, he inched long, strong fingers up her legs, cupping and squeezing, until he reached her upper thighs. The heated satiny texture of the skin at the back of her legs invited him to explore further.

Bethany's hands remained braced against him, fingers curled, nails digging into his chest, and a low moan eased between her parted lips as her head fell back, pushing her breasts against the front of her blouse. Her nipples enticed, beckoned, from behind the dark silk. Pulling his hands from the warmth of her skin under the slacks, Jonathan continued his quest.

இஇஇ

305

She wanted to protest when his fingers left off stroking beneath the silk. But she had no breath left, as he moved immediately to claim the uncovered skin at her throat. One deft hand cupped her neck under the silk, while a marauding finger eased along the crossed opening, almost but not quite sliding underneath.

"Jonathan?" she asked, when his hand rested there against the wild tumult of her heartbeat.

"Remember, Bethany, I want only what you want to give me."

So, it had come to this. Her blood was singing and her breath would barely pull into her lungs and she wasn't sure if she would ever stop shaking. It was delightfully obvious he was in no better shape. Still, the next step, the big step, was up to her.

Slowly, she shifted her weight from her hands to her thighs. Her fingers played with the buttons at her waist, then chickened out, releasing the cuffs first. Pulled by the heavy silver buttons, the sleeves fell open to the shoulder. Only by a faint tightening of his mouth did he rebuke her cowardice. Then her fingers slid to her waist once more and before she could change her mind again, they had eased the silver through the openings, and the blouse was held on her body only by the stiffening points of her nipples.

The dark green silk fell open, framing her body. If he wondered how much braver she would get, he'd apparently decided not to wait to find out. Slowly, keeping eye contact the whole time, he slid his hands down her chest, reaching for what the blouse still concealed.

His hands fit perfectly around her. Her nipples arched against his palms while his fingers spanned the sides of her breast. A gasp caught in her throat, and she leaned into his hands, her chest rising and falling abruptly with her sudden panting breaths.

The slight callouses on his warm palm sent bolts of sensation into her toes and to the top of her head. She didn't know how it could get any better. Then he pulled her forward, raised his head, and her nipple disappeared into his mouth. Seeing his lips against her breast, watching his cheeks draw in slightly as she felt the suction drag at her tender skin was so erotic she bit her lip to stifle her moan.

"Stop that," he whispered urgently, lifting his mouth only enough to form the words against her nipple. "Are you trying to drive me totally mad?" Then his mouth closed again in a delicate love bite.

"I'm the one going crazy," she whispered urgently. "Jonathan!"

❧❧

"Moan, scream, beg," he commanded, sliding his mouth across her chest while his hand covered the damp nipple. "I want to hear every last little sound."

"What am I supposed to beg for?"

Her voice was suddenly cold, distant, and he cursed his careless phrasing. He stroked along her back, soothing her, bringing her closer. "Bad choice of words, precious. I'm a photographer, I can only see the way I want the picture to develop. You tell me what to do, where you want my mouth and my hands. Demand."

Her fingers plunged into his hair, tugging him away from her breast.

"Kiss me," she demanded, in a passion thickened voice as she brought his mouth under hers in an energetic meeting of tongue and lip and tooth. "Now, stop listening to my nonsense and get on with this seduction!"

Had he ever laughed so much during intimacy as he did with this woman? He certainly couldn't remember when. While his chest still shook with laughter, he put her hands on the buttons of his shirt, and urged her to open them. For once, she did something without hesitation or argument and was soon stroking through his chest hair as though she reveled in the sensations.

Bethany might have seen many bare chests, but she'd obviously never been encouraged to stroke and study one. She accepted the invitation eagerly, running her fingers through his chest hairs. Then she found his nipples, already lifting up and begging for the attention hers had received. Without hesitation, she bent forward, her breasts rubbing along his stomach as she took his nipple gently between her teeth.

"Bethany, *yes*!" He half rose off the couch. "Precious, don't stop now." Fingers delving deep into her unbound hair, he rubbed her scalp while guiding her across his chest. Then he felt her mouth and hands begin to travel further down, and he pushed slightly at her head, not wanting to lose total control of the situation.

When she rose this time, the blouse fell off one shoulder. A quick shrug disposed of it completely. She sat very still as though waiting for any comment, her only covering the hair that had strayed over her shoulders. Then she tossed her head, doing great damage to what little was left of his self-control, and the hair was out of his way.

"Does this bother you, precious?" he asked in a very low voice. Seeing her frown of non-comprehension, he smiled gently. "Being looked at. Does it bother you?"

"No, not when you look at me," she admitted softly.

"Good." It was beyond good. She was separating this from her past. "Because I want to look at you. All of you."

He slid his hands down her body, stopping to visit with her nipples while she rested against her fingers spread through his chest hair. Then he was spanning her waist, stroking down the outside of her thighs, sliding under the silk, cupping her knees. Gentle encouragement spread her legs further apart until she nestled intimately against the eager waiting heat of him.

There was a rightness to this that defied all description. Eyes squeezed shut in sensual delight, Bethany relaxed her lower body, striving to get as close as possible. It was still not enough. Without conscious thought, her fingers flew to her waistband, releasing the luxurious silver buttons. As the material fell away she was reaching for him, stretching her legs out along his, sliding her fingers into his hair as her breasts crushed against his chest and their mouths fused. Still, it was not enough.

She was melting against him, her tongue desperately seeking newly learned intimacies. Her nipples burned against his chest. Now, when he stroked down her back, when he cupped her derriere and held her locked to him, he felt only heated silken skin beneath his hands. He shifted, rolling until she was nestled between his body and the back of the couch. Gasping, he forced his mouth off hers, tasting and nibbling down her neck. In a last uncertainty, a last flare of caretaking, he raised his head. He knew, when she opened her eyes, she would first see an aroused male, looming over her, outlined by a firelight that could only make him seem more menacing.

Her eyes did open, hazy, the pupils expanded from her intense need. For a moment, she merely looked at him, then she smiled. A wide, witching smile. Her fingers traced his ear, stroked down his neck, meandered along his shoulders and foraged further. With no shyness now, she found his nipple, stroked it, flicked it with her short nails. When he reacted with a hissing groan, the smile broadened, revealing even white teeth clamped around her tongue.

"Jonathan?" There was no hesitation in her low, sultry voice, only blatant invitation.

"Bethany," he whispered, making her name a word of great beauty. His hand lifted, stroking the wild beauty of her hair back from her face. "Precious, are you protected?"

It took a full minute for his question to penetrate her passion fogged mind. Then the body nestled so warmly intimate against his went coldly still. In that instant he realized what a fatal error in judgment he had made. Before he could open his mouth to retract the question, flaming color had rushed into her face.

"Oh, Jonathan, I..."

"Of course you aren't," he muttered, disgusted with his own insensitivity. "I shouldn't have had to ask." He captured the graceful hand that had frozen against his chest and kissed it softly before beginning to pull away from her.

Wrenching her hand from his tender hold, Bethany grasped his shoulder. "Jonathan, no, don't leave." There was a desperate note in her voice that tore at his heart. "I'm sorry. It doesn't matter."

"It does matter," he said firmly, leaning down for a quick, soft kiss before sitting up and sliding his arms around her. "And I'm not leaving." He rose, holding her high against his chest. The emerald silk fell away, and her hair swung free. "We're merely adjourning to another room."

He gazed at her body, golden in the firelight. Tenderly, he pressed his lips to her brow, her cheek, her mouth. Shifting her slightly, he lifted her higher, and once more tasted her pouting nipple.

"I feel like a conquering hero, carrying off the greatest of all prizes. You are every fantasy I ever had."

Mona Karel

The well-built fire lit an empty room, a flare of deep green on the carpet and a firmly closed bedroom door.

CHAPTER 14

Bethany stifled a moan of pleasure. The warmth from the fireplace followed them into Jonathan's room, keeping the chill from their overheated bodies. Jonathan carried her in, pushing the door closed behind him and stopping, his back leaned against the door. She lay quietly in his arms for a moment then stirred, insecurity working its way up through her layers of contentment.

"Jonathan? What's wrong?"

"Nothing, precious. Not one thing in the world. I'm just standing here, enjoying the feel of you in my arms."

She sighed, snuggling closer as his arms tightened around her.

"I seem to be faced with a dilemma, though."

"What's that?"

"I have to lay you down long enough to take my pants off."

"That makes sense."

"Of course, it does. I just don't want to be separated from you that long."

The only reply she could manage was a nervous chuckle. This kind of sensual teasing was new, and she wasn't quite sure how to respond. Jonathan's arms were hard and strong around her, and he held her safely against his chest. She could feel his heart beating against hers. It was a brand new tactile experience for her and she intended to explore it to the utmost.

She intended to enjoy all of it, and to store it in her memory in a series of erotic prints. What Jonathan had done for her might not seem romantic to everyone. He hadn't presented her with fabulous gifts or paraded her around town. He actually hadn't even given her flowers. All of these things she knew to be the trappings of romance.

Jonathan gave her the gift of her own worth. He had tended not only to her body but also to her soul, her psyche, or whatever it was that set her apart from every other female who had ever yearned after his warm blue eyes. For that, if nothing else, she was supremely grateful.

So much more was going on, though. Finally pushing himself away from the door, he moved across the dimly lit room to his huge, raised bed. There wasn't much of a moon tonight, but the stars, looking down on them through the skylight, bathed the bed in silky light.

His bed was large, and firm under the thick quilt. Much like him, it offered support and comfort. He propped her on an upraised knee, then turned down one side of the bed and slid her between the sheets. With obvious reluctance, he covered her against the chill.

Bethany looked away from him, absorbing the impact of the room while trying to come to terms with herself. This was it. She had, of her own free will, chosen to be in this bed. It felt a bit frightening and very, very right.

Never taking his eyes from her covered form in his bed, Jonathan dropped off his shirt, stepped out of his shoes and slacks. For the moment, he left his briefs on. He slid into the bed, reaching for her. She lay still, looking up at the stars putting on a show for them from light years away. For just a moment, she resisted his hand, then something seemed to

317

let go inside her. With a tiny sound, she nestled against him, coming home to his arms.

Yes. This was right. This roughness against sensitive skin, this heat to heat, escalating to near frightening proportions. This touching, this holding. This love. Tonight, when he gave so much to her, not taking for himself although she could feel the trembling ache in his body, she admitted her love. Whatever else life brought her, for this night, she could admit to the world and herself that she loved Jonathan.

Bethany's thoughts tumbled feverishly around in her head as she tried to burrow closer to his side. He reached down, pulling her leg up over his, her inner thigh brushing against the slight cotton restraint he still wore. Nothing in her past had prepared her for the erotic delight of feeling her most private, most female part pressed against powerful thigh muscles. Nor could she have ever imagined how it felt to have her bare skin stroked by large, strong hands.

He used no practiced moves. There were no subtle nudges at known erogenous zones, nor did he grab at her intimate areas. Instead, he stroked her hair, her back, her waist, his hands moving in ceaseless patterns of pleasure. Then he cupped her derriere, sliding his fingers into the separation of her cheeks, squeezing so gently, so softly. She remembered what he had said, about her rear driving him crazy, and she arched against him.

"You like that?" he murmured, pulling her even closer to him. A fine sheen of perspiration covered his chest now, and she could feel the thunder of his heartbeat under her cheek. Daring, she turned her head, burrowing her face into his chest hair, setting her lips carefully on his chest.

"Yes, precious," he whispered, lacing his fingers through her hair. "Touch me."

"Where? How?"

"Anywhere, any way you want."

Emboldened by his permission, she raised herself on an elbow, until just the sensitive tip of her nipple touched his chest. For a moment she hesitated, letting the fascinating sensations distract her. But there was too much to explore, and not enough time.

Pushing back the covers, she inspected the alien territory of his body. His chest she knew now, at least part of it, although he made interesting sounds when she flicked gently at a hidden nipple with her finger. There was a faint trace of rib under his lean muscled torso, and the hard warmth of his stomach delighted her fingers.

The waistband of his dark blue briefs stopped her, and she looked up. He had propped a pillow under his head, and was watching with a semblance of ease, although stress was pulling in the corners of his mouth. Still, his hands stroked through her hair, gently tracing her ear and stroking the side of her neck.

"Go ahead, baby. Whatever you want to do."

Encouraged, she slid the tips of her fingers under the elastic waistband, following the path of coarse hair. Then her fingers encountered softer hair, and hot, satiny skin. She continued to explore, until she touched the throbbing heat of him, until she felt his life force against her palm. Gaining courage by the second, she dared to cup him, to stroke along his length and measure him against her hand.

He surged, his masculine hardness a living entity in her hands. Jonathan had given to her, taking nothing for himself, and it showed in the sharp moan that slipped out between his clenched teeth. Acting on instinct, she trailed kisses down his damp skin, tasting salt and desperation as she ventured into unknown territory.

"Lift up," she whispered, pushing at the overstrained briefs.

The starlight glowed along his rigid shaft, highlighting the single drop at the tip. Reaching out slowly, Bethany touched just the end of one finger to the moisture. His hands clenched in her hair, almost to the point of hurting. She looked up, meeting the intense glitter of his eyes, as she delicately inserted the tip of her finger between her lips, tasting his essence.

Hungry for more, she pulled against his hold, reaching out her tongue to taste him directly in an intimacy she had never before considered. Now, it seemed so very right.

❧❧❧

Jonathan felt his insides tense beyond bearing. Bethany's shy, inexpert touch was sending him over the edge, but he couldn't bear to stop her. Until she opened her sweet lips, preparing to take all of him into the damp heat of her mouth.

"No, baby. Not this time."

He pushed at her head, using his hands in her hair to keep her from the contact he so desperately wanted. It had been too long and he had wanted her too desperately to trust himself.

She looked up, confusion warring with the sensual lethargy in her shadowed eyes. Releasing her hair, he trailed a finger along her chin, behind her neck, using the leverage to draw her mouth up to his. Before she could protest, he pulled her closer, until their bodies touched, for the first time, with no barriers.

Rolling over on top of her, he propped himself up on his elbows, wanting to feel her but not wanting to intimidate her with his weight. The sensations were beyond description and he flexed his hips, torturing himself just a little bit more. Gasping, he reached for the drawer.

Her eyes were large and solemn in the sparse light, but there was a tense feel to her body. Fumbling one-handed with the box he'd forgotten to open earlier, he gently stroked back her hair. "What's wrong, precious?"

She shrugged first, that irritating, charming habit she had when she didn't quite know how to say something. Then a deep breath moved her dangerously against him. "You seem to be well-stocked, this far out in the woods."

"You can thank the powers that be for small town pharmacies that aren't totally repressed. If we had to rely on my old supplies, we'd be dealing with potential calamity."

Success at last. Smiling with a tremendous effort, he held the small packet up. There was a new twinkle in her fascinating eyes, a devastating expression of relief and mischief. She didn't speak, but a small hand stroked along his chin, fingers tracing over his mouth, probing between his teeth. He opened his mouth, sucking her fingers in, stroking with his tongue. Then he levered himself away from her.

"Here, precious." He eased the small packet into her damp fingers. "You do the honors."

Exercising control he didn't know he had, he sat up, letting his hands rest on his tense thighs. She studied the package, pulling the edges apart, letting the contents fall into her palm. Her gaze lowered, ever so slowly, to the obvious appendage that waited, not so patiently now, to be covered.

"Now is not the time to play silly games, Bethany."

露

His voice was more strained than she'd ever heard it before. Moving more quickly now, she smoothed the covering over his waiting hardness, wondering at the catch in his breath when she took an extra moment to touch, gently, the heavy roundness below. Then she felt her hips tilt upward.

"Yes," he breathed, as he eased down against her, bracing himself against his hands. "Bring me home, sweetheart."

She guided him, participating in all ways with this act of absolute love. Whatever happened, Jonathan would receive pleasure from her body. She owed that much to him.

He was hard and hot, stretching her in ways she'd never known before. Suddenly all thoughts of merely allowing Jonathan pleasure were gone. Bracing her heels against the bed, Bethany lifted herself to him, seeking, demanding more.

Jonathan felt the exultant laughter rising within him, as he fought to govern himself for as long as possible. From gentle maiden, she'd turned wanton, pressing her head into the pillow, offering herself in total abandon. Abandoning all thoughts of gentlemanly restraint, he lowered his weight fully against her, and lost control right along with her, plunging into the sweet oblivion of love.

೦౨೦౨

Bethany eased the battered motorhome to a stop at the entrance to the interstate. The golden days were over. It was raining, torrents of water streaming down the windshield. The wipers were at full speed, the defroster was turned on high. But nothing could wipe out the tears that were not falling, the fog in her heart. Bethany wondered if she was making the worst decision of her life.

He'd been sprawled across the bed when she left that morning, after a nearly sleepless night. At first the wakefulness had been mutual and intimate. Then she'd been tucked securely against his side and he melted around her into utter boneless exhaustion. They'd explored each other in passion and caring and it was light years removed from any former experience. But she hadn't been able to sleep. Replete, her cravings for the moment appeased, she lay in his arms, pressed up against his side, loving every minute of it and knowing she could not stay.

She'd been his fantasy, and he had fulfilled that fantasy. He had known the virgin bride, the mystery woman. If she stayed, would it have been as the happy teenager, the confused bride or the emotionally injured woman? Whatever, it would become an incomplete image she was trying to project, for his sake. Reality would have eventually made demands and there would be a failure she didn't think she could survive.

She looked at the hated car phone, wanting to hear his voice for a minute. He would worry, but she could send a message through Neil. If she called now—well, she didn't think she was far enough away from him yet. He would want to talk about it. He would come up with so many reasons why she should stay, and she would only have one reason why she should go. It was what she had to do.

She'd been so many people, for so long, none of them completely her. She needed to be away, alone, and become herself. It would be so very easy to become Jonathan's friend, and maybe more. But she'd be offering only a part of herself, and he deserved so much more. When she came to him, she would bring a total woman, and hope it would be enough.

When she was with him, her emotions were too raw, too close to the surface and she couldn't think clearly. She had to get away, to pull the parts of herself into a cohesive unit. Fulfilling his fantasy had fulfilled so many of hers, but staying could destroy her, unless she was ready to take the final step. She had to be able to face the world on her own, as a complete woman, before she was ready to face him again.

The decision made, she considered her available options. She wouldn't go to any of her convenient stops. This she needed to do for herself, by herself. She eyed the telephone again. Reaching for it, she resolutely punched out a series of numbers.

"Marsha? It's Bethany Acton. Right, BL Acton. It's what time? I'm sorry. No, I don't want to talk to Neil. You can go back to sleep, just tell me: Where did you get that lovely green outfit?"

※※※

She was gone. He didn't need to reach out to know the bed was cold and empty next to him. The sun had crept stealthily across most of the bed, finally touching his face and waking him gently. He wished it had still been raining. It wasn't right to be bathed in sunlight and be alone. They should have been falling asleep again, in a wet tangle after another session of loving.

He wasn't going to bother to check the other rooms or the parking area. She was gone. The house was deserted, quiet, echoing in its emptiness. There would be no more wet-footed red clown greeting him. No more hiking companions, no more breakfast buddies. No more Bethany.

He rolled over onto his back, arm blocking out the obnoxiously cheerful sun. Had he rushed her? Had he hurt her? He remembered her face, frozen in excruciating pleasure, her legs wrapped around his waist, trying desperately to draw him even closer. She'd found pleasure the night before and, he was sure, contentment. If he'd stayed awake, would she have left? But he could not have held her there, any more than he'd been able to tame and hold the wild animals. She had to want to stay on her own.

Feeling he needed to do something, he reached for the telephone then stopped himself. Every time she faced an overload of emotion she'd gone away, and he'd gone after her. This time, she had to come back on her own.

Satisfied with his decision, he swung himself out of bed. He had a critical gallery showing in a month. He had orders to fill, projects to plan. He had a myriad of things to take care of that had been neglected recently. He didn't have time to worry about her.

He would give her one month. After the showing, he was going after her.

The beautiful people were out in full force, eyeing each other's apparel, comparing jewelry and hairstyles. Artificial smiles accompanied insincere greetings and empty platitudes, and everyone was happy to be where they could be seen. From time to time they also looked at the exquisitely displayed photographs.

The drink in his hand sported a melting ice cube. Jonathan tolerated the people, as he had tolerated the uninvited critics and the gushing art groupies. This was the most crowded opening ever held of his work, proving the worth of the printed word.

In a departure from his past showings, he had sought out publicity for this one. As a result, in addition to the people who appreciated photography as an art form, there were people attending simply because this had been proclaimed the place to be tonight. He hadn't enjoyed seeking the publicity, nor was he delighted with all the results. But if he expected Bethany to abandon the habits formed by her memories, he would have to learn to open himself up to the scrutiny of the masses.

Not all those attending were unwelcome. Neil was there with his wife Marsha, and most of the staff of *Western Living*. Except for one obstreperous, irritating, beloved writer. All Neil would say was what he'd been saying for one long, miserable month. Bethany was doing well, and would be at the opening.

Jonathan had chosen not to read the interview before it was printed. Trust was a major part of this decision. He had to trust that Bethany would write fairly and with candor. She had written brilliantly, and with what he wanted to believe was love. It was all that got him through what had to be the worst month of his life. That, and believing she had to be as unhappy as he was.

Activity at the entrance drew his attention. Obviously late arrivals, planning to make an appearance. Noting the elegance of their attire, he began to turn away, but stopped as they stepped into the brighter light away from the door. The woman was cloaked from head to toe in flowing dark green silk. She reached slender hands up to lower the hood, revealing a styled mass of auburn hair. As she reached for the fastening of the cape, she smiled up at her escort, a blond man of exceptional masculine beauty. Jonathan wondered who Paul had found to escort, and how soon would it be before he would need Bethany to get rid of her.

The woman swirled the cape off her shoulders with a practiced turn of her wrist, and passed it into the man's care. The outfit revealed was of a finer, softer silk—a dark emerald green top, fastened at the waist and cuffs by cast silver buttons. The pale ivory skirt was made up of flowing layers of silk.

∾∾

Bethany handed her cape to Paul, cautioning herself not to look around, not to pay attention to the people paying an inordinate amount of attention to her. "I feel like I'm on exhibition. What's going on here?" Her lightness was forced as she allowed one fleeting glance down at herself. Everything was still where it belonged. "Do you always draw this kind of attention, Paul?"

"I somehow doubt the scrutiny is for me," Paul said quietly, his brilliant green eyes making an intense survey of her appearance. "Where have you been all this time?" His voice didn't rise above a strained whisper.

"Are you all right? You look..." she hesitated, not able to find the exact phrase to describe his stunned expression.

"Completely bowled over. No wonder you wanted to meet me in the hotel lobby." He handed the elegant cape over to an attendant then laid a hand lightly on her elbow, turning her to look her over completely. "Three years, and I never saw it."

"Paul?" For just a moment, she allowed her attention to be diverted to her friend. "Is something wrong?"

He expelled a deep, heavy breath and laid his other hand on her shoulder. Then he released her elbow, and touched her cheek, stroking one finger slowly toward her hair. Bethany kept herself still as long as she could then edged away. Her hair, loosely styled to frame tense, delicate features, lifted and fell with the nervous toss of her head.

Paul smiled grimly to himself. "I never saw it in three years. He saw it in three minutes." His voice held the sad tones of someone who has lost a great treasure before knowing they possessed it. "Do you need me for anything else?" he asked, voice brisk once more, the ultimate bachelor friend escort.

"No," she said, reaching for the core of strength within herself. "I have to do this alone." She dared for the first time to look around, to meet the multitude of curious eyes.

"Just so you know, pretty lady, your boss and co-workers are over to your left. The main attraction was glaring an icy hole in my back a few minutes ago. He's over to your right, pretending to hold a serious discussion with a woman in beads, leather, and purple hair." His forced whimsy faded as he once more laid a gentle hand on her shoulder. "He was watching the door when we came in."

"I know." She always knew when Jonathan was looking at her. And she had seen the expression on his face when he looked away. "Thanks for everything, Paul. I think I'll look around first."

❧❧❧

Paul watched her glide away, completely at ease on the insubstantial heels, head at a regal angle, back majestically straight. She took a flute of champagne from a passing waiter and, delicately tasting the bubbling wine, drifted to her left, examining the displays, ignoring the people.

Obtaining a different glass from the same waiter, Paul lifted the scotch in her direction, a silent toast to what had never been.

❧❧

"Acton? Marsha said you'd been busy but..." Seemingly at a loss for words for the first time in all the years Bethany had known him, Neil shook his head and stared. Then he smiled, a huge slash of white across his lined face, and his arms enveloped her in an expansive hug. "You look fabulous."

Bethany suffered the hug, stepping away as soon as she could without seeming rude. Before she could find her voice Marsha, the consummate mother and hostess, stepped in to offer a breezy cheek press.

"You needn't sound so surprised, Neil. Bethany has always presented herself in accord with her circumstances. This is the first time she's appeared as a celebrity in her own right. That style is charming, dear." She lightly touched Bethany's hair, smoothing away some of the wildness. "You were right, it would not have looked near as lovely pinned up."

"What do you mean, celebrity?" Still not accustomed to being touched and petted in public, Bethany held herself absolutely still. It was strange being mothered and fussed over. Not bad, just strange.

The older couple exchanged what had to be a guilty look, but were saved from having to explain their cryptic words by the influx of magazine staff. Suddenly, everyone seemed to remember how well they had gotten along with BL Acton, and how closely they had worked together. She took it all in her stride, sipping delicately at the champagne, casting surreptitious glances around the room. Once the uproar settled, she turned to her boss.

"Okay, Neil, what's going on?"

He didn't pretend to not understand her. "The article was one of your best ever, Acton. I'm sorry we couldn't get hold of you to approve the layout." As he spoke, he drew her away from the group of co-workers, toward a table featuring a display of *Western Living* magazines.

"You've never needed me to approve in the past." She accepted the proffered issue, noting the cover illustration was of the golden eagle riding thermals over the tree tops. A colored clip marked the article, and she opened the magazine to a menacing portrait of a wolf on the tundra, protecting its young.

There was no need to read the words. They were ingrained on her heart, her only company for many sleepless hours alone in her motorhome. Neil had assured her they had only added captions for the illustrations sent by Jonathan. These were among his finest work, most seen here for the first time. Then she turned the page.

A side-bar, accented by a background color of soft green, was entitled "About the Author." The accompanying illustration was a portrait of her in jungle fatigues, battered cap perched on her casually pinned-up hair. She'd been photographed leaning against a huge fallen tree, looking up from scribbling in a notebook. Baron was perched on the tree next to her, obviously about to leap off in search of something else he couldn't catch.

Neil's by-line was on the side bar, a glowing account of her work for *Western Living*, and a brief history of her and her dog. Bethany read it carefully, twice, and looked a long time at the photograph. She couldn't decide which one of them she was more irritated with, but Neil was more convenient. He was also her boss.

"Before you erupt," Neil interjected, rescuing the magazine from her clenching grasp, "Let me tell you that I intended to present you sometime this past year. The time never seemed quite right to bring it up. For now, I want you to go over there," he indicated a section in the gallery that had been designed to form a small cubicle. "Look in there with an open mind."

Once again, she crossed the room alone, feeling like she was the center of attention. It was a delusion, of course. There was no reason for this sophisticated group to have more than a cursory interest in her. No matter how revealing the sidebar illustration had been, she knew she was light years away from that woman. Tonight, anyway.

The cubicle contained an exclusive display of photographs, with the legend: "From the Private Collection of J. Phillip Merritt, NOT FOR SALE." There was work from his early years, at home and in Europe. There were special, whimsical, photos of young deer learning to walk and squirrels cavorting in the trees. Mostly, there were photographs of her.

No wonder everyone acted as though they knew her. She was displayed from every angle, in every phase of the change made while she stayed at his house. There was even a close up of a teenage girl, her hair flying to the side as she laughed into the camera. Bethany tried to dredge up a good flaming anger, but could only look, in awe, at the presentation of herself as a beautiful woman. Was this, also, a private man's public demonstration of caring? She stiffened. She would know soon.

"That was someone I knew once." The voice at her elbow was without emotion, or so overloaded with emotion, words were not an adequate means of expression.

"She's quite lovely in these photos." All her new-found courage was deserting her. She did not dare turn and meet the anger she knew would be in his cool eyes.

"I thought she was in life, in all the ways that mattered. But it never developed."

Had she been able to hear over the breaking of her own heart, Bethany might have heard the pain Jonathan hid so poorly.

Wounded, she made a last stand, turning slightly to look in his direction. "Perhaps you used the wrong process."

"Perhaps," he said, noncommittally. "Perhaps there was not as much there to work with as I once believed."

The display that had seemed an expression of affection was now seen to be a demonstration of a master's skill. She turned away, noticing that the lights seemed to be dimmed, giving an underwater effect to the room. Still, she should be able to find Paul or Neil without too much trouble. It would have been much better for her to not have come tonight.

CHAPTER 15

Jonathan laid a hand on her arm, biting in above her elbow. Flinching from his touch as she attempted to leave the cubicle, she was pushed off balance. The elegant shoes became a sudden liability and she stumbled.

"Oh, for God's sake. What have you got on your feet?"

His grip became steadying, both hands holding her arms as his gaze disapproved of the insubstantial shoes. Painted toenails peeked at him from between dainty straps holding an impossibly high heel in place. He turned his attention to the full silk skirt, a fragile shade of ivory, then stopped looking when he got to the emerald blouse.

"Damn you, did you have to wear that blouse?" He hadn't meant to say it. He'd meant to be calm and cool, to congratulate her on her new look. He was an adult, he could tolerate occasional rejection. Then he looked up to her face and saw her eyes, made brilliant by unshed tears, the only color in a face drained of life.

When she would have wrenched away, he cursed at her, at himself, at life. His hold tightened, pulling her away from the engrossed gallery crowd and into a small, plush office lit by one lamp. Here he released her, letting her hide herself in a darker corner.

છ૭છ૭

"Congratulations. It seems your showing is a success," she said, very properly, through shivering teeth. Away from the crush of people, she was suddenly chilled. Certainly it was only the reduced temperature causing her to quake.

"No thanks to you. I lost nearly a week worrying about you. Dammit, why did you leave?"

"You got your fantasy, Jonathan. It wouldn't have worked out beyond that."

"So you decided it wouldn't work, and just snuck off into the night. That's a coward's way out."

"Fine, so I'm a coward." She spoke to the wall, wondering how much longer she was going to have to stay here. How many times had her attacks of cowardice ruined her life? How many times had she run rather than face up to a problem, how many times had she given in rather than refusing? When would it be time to face her fears and move on? Her cowardly fingers made it to the buttons on her cuffs, releasing them so that the sleeves fell open to the shoulders. Her lightly tanned arms were bare, chilling quickly in the cool air.

"What's this?" his voice sneered from across the room. "Want one more toss before you go? Sorry, sweetie, I don't do quickies." He sounded utterly bored, almost contemptuous.

Her fingers fumbled then moved to the buttons at her waist. Behind her, she could hear him stirring, as though about to leave the room. Drawing a deep breath, she moved forward into the light, releasing the buttons, opening the blouse before her nerve deserted her. A shrug of her shoulders let it slide off in one smooth move, ending up draped elegantly from one hand.

"So," he said, his voice colder than she had heard it before. "You've had a taste of passion and want some more. What's wrong? Is golden boy boring in bed?"

She shuddered then raised her chin again.

"I thought maybe..." All of her half plans and wistful dreams of a happy ending suddenly seemed pathetic. Jonathan may have been briefly interested in the fact that she was able to wear white again, in such a revealing outfit. She was still too flawed—not enough woman to hold him for a long term commitment.

"You thought I would take one look at you in that sexy outfit, not be able to keep my hands off you, and we could start up where we left off."

Said like that, in his tense, angry-sounding voice, her grand scheme sounded juvenile and manipulative. Bethany gave up, letting her shoulders slump as she turned to the door, fumbling to pull the blouse back on.

"Sorry. This was stupid. I should have known better."

ఆసౌ

Jonathan let her get as far as the door. Then he moved quickly, coming up behind her as she reached out a trembling hand to the knob. He doubted she could see much through the tears he was sure were swimming in her eyes.

"Why stupid?" he asked, gently taking hold of her bare shoulders. "When you were so very right?"

With a slight yearning sound, she let herself be turned around and cradled against his chest. Seeing the bumps raising on her bare arms, Jonathan flicked open the buttons of his jacket. It was simple to guide her hands into the warmth trapped between his shirt and jacket, and he could hold her that much closer against his aching body.

"I was going to wake you up that morning from the inside out. I wanted to make love to you, watching the sunshine caress your skin. I wanted to hear you scream with ecstasy in the middle of the afternoon—and you left, dammit!"

"Your fantasy was fulfilled. I left before you got tired of me." She obviously tried very hard to sound matter-of-fact.

"My fantasy?"

"The mystery girl, the virgin bride. Unfulfilled desires—old fascinations—temptations resisted. That sort of thing."

"You thought that was my fantasy?"

"You said you wanted me."

"I wanted—I want—all of you. I want Bethany Louise Acton, writer extraordinaire, companion of my days, tormenter of my nights. Why didn't you stay and talk to me?" He was still angry about her desertion, and still holding her as closely as he could.

She shrugged as much as she could while nestled in his arms. "I had to leave," she said, rubbing her cheek against his chest. "I had to be more than just a clinging female. You were always tending me, always taking care of me. You thought I was weak—"

"You? Weak?" He cut her off, thinking of her indomitable will, her irritating strength of mind. "Not hardly. A weak woman would never have made something out of the nothing your life was. You were a Phoenix rising from the ashes of that damned yacht. I only wish you could have let me rise with you." He held her away from his body, trying to make her see in his face what she refused to hear in his voice. "I took care of you because I wanted to.

I hoped one day you would want to reciprocate. Many times."

He felt the tightness ease in himself as he took in her changed appearance. Her hair was styled to be a windblown frame for her face. She wore subtle make-up, fragile gold earrings, oh-so-delicate scent. Her hand lifted, as though reaching out to the lines he could feel imbedded on his face.

Jonathan took the hand in his. The callouses still there were smoothed over, and she had obviously not stinted on hand creams. Elegant nails, polished in a subtle bronze shade, graced the ends of her fingers. He raised the hand to his mouth, taking one finger between his lips, then slid his tongue under her nail, pushing gently.

Bethany's body softened against him, trusting her weight to the strength of his arm behind her. Her breathing deepened.

"You look so wonderful," he said hoarsely, staring at her now damp finger. Then his eyes lifted, meeting the alluring haze of hers. "Was this all for me?"

"No," she said with a small smile. "It was all for me."

He met the smile with an uninhibited grin, bringing her hand to rest on his shoulder while he reached out to stroke along her neck. His hand spread suddenly, possessively, across her chest, his palm pushing at the top of her bodice.

"And this? Is this for you?"

Hazy green eyes locked on his face, Bethany slid her other hand out from its warm nest behind his back, reaching under her arm. A slight lift of her manicured fingers, and the bodice relaxed its hold.

Jonathan's grin faded as he watched the downward progression of the shirred silk. It stopped at the rise of her breasts, above the nipples but below the subtle tan line. He traced the tan line with one finger, pushing down the bodice further, reaching under to stroke an eager, lonely nipple. Then her breath caught, shifting the bodice, and he slid his hand down and around her breast, lifting it to his mouth.

He felt her body jolt as his tongue rasped over her swollen nipple, cherishing the tender skin. Her nails dug into his shoulder, letting her body arch backward over his arm, apparently trusting his strength. Then his hand stroked lower, cupping her waist, reaching for the derriere that continued to fascinate him.

"This skirt," she managed to gasp. "Marsha helped me find it. It was designed by the same person—" She clutched desperately at his head, sliding her fingers through his hair. "—as the blouse."

Jonathan smiled around her nipple, understanding perfectly. His hand sifted through the layers of delicate silk, finding a more precious treasure underneath. Loose silk tap pants covered her heated body, enhancing his touch. He raised his head to look down at the woman in his arms.

The silk had divided to expose her long, tanned leg. She lay back, her arms looped loosely around his neck. Her damp nipple was begging to return to its warm lodging, her eyes were bright with desire and trust.

"You're lucky you're wearing something under this, young lady." His fingers pressed luxuriously into the skin under the delicate silk, cupping her derriere and pulling her even closer.

"That is not an unalterable situation, sir," she said primly.

His laughter cut through the tension between them. "Not here, precious. This gallery is only open a few more hours. I have plans that will take at least a week to carry out."

He slid his hand out reluctantly from under the skirt and cradled her against him. "Just stay here a second. It was so damned lonely on that mountain top without you."

ↄ⌒ↄ⌒ↄ

Bethany allowed herself to nestle against him. Whatever the future would bring, right now Jonathan needed her, and she could not deny him.

The first knock was so soft, neither of them consciously heard it. It was repeated, a bit louder, then the door opened just enough to admit one tall man.

"Is everything all—I see it is. About time you two came to your senses." Paul's gentle chiding did not quite mask the concern in his voice. He looked appreciatively at the intimate scene.

"What the hell do you want?" Jonathan snarled, not loosening his hold.

"What I want is immaterial. There's some Frenchman out here claiming to be Beth's husband."

Bethany stiffened, attempting to pull away from Jonathan's protective embrace. "I'll need to—"

"You'll need to stay still for a minute, woman." Jonathan refused to ease the tension in his arms. "Paul, get out of here."

Instead of obeying, Paul strolled leisurely toward them. He reached down to the floor, picking up a flow of dark green silk. It dangled from one finger.

"Lose something?" he asked mildly.

At the sound of the voice behind her, Bethany stopped trying to pull away from Jonathan. Instead, she tried to bury herself closer to the protection of his jacket. She didn't see the look that passed between the two men as Paul laid the blouse on a chair.

"I'll be right outside."

Once the door closed quietly behind Paul, she moved away from Jonathan, reaching for the sagging bodice. Somehow, she couldn't quite get her fingers to cooperate on the hooks this time. It took a minute to realize her hands were shaking.

"Hold this for a minute." Jonathan pushed the blouse into her fumbling fingers. He positioned her in front of him, all business as he set about putting her in order. Before he lifted the bodice to cover her enticing flesh, he leaned over to kiss each breast, lingering on her nipples. "I do love your sexy outfit, precious, but these are my goodies."

Even through the sudden chill of fear that had overcome her, Bethany managed a small smile. It became even broader as she allowed him to dress her like a fashion doll. He was very serious about manipulating the tiny hooks, then arranging the green silk blouse, not letting her do anything.

"Just stand there and look beautiful. I like you in a state of shock. You seem to be quieter. Maybe my true calling is as a dresser of gorgeous women. It's almost as much fun as undressing them."

It was all nonsense, of course, meant to make her feel less worried. Then he was straightening her hair, touching her cheek.

"All right now?"

"Just a minute. Now it's your turn." She pulled his tailored jacket closed, straightening the collar and fastening the buttons. The intimacy of the act stunned her. But there was no time to explore that now.

Paul waited immediately outside the door, leaning against the wall. He fell into step on Bethany's right side, slightly behind her as they moved across the floor. The crowd watched her more closely than ever, but her attention was elsewhere.

ഇൟ**ഇ**

Bethany felt Jonathan's arm tighten under her hand and heard his sudden gasp. Then they were across the room.

Stefan Dubec stood by the alcove of private work. Even now, he was a man of bearing and distinction, and he was not alone. A dark-haired woman, elegantly dressed, stood near his shoulder. Her designer original gown and jewelry had probably cost almost as much as the magic that gave her an unlined face.

"So, Phillip," the woman said, drawling his name. Her accent was extreme. When she was young, she might have even been attractive. "You finally got the little virgin. Oh, I forget. She's not a virgin now, is she?"

"It is enough, Marlene," Stefan said sharply, his English heavily accented. "I allowed you to come only if you behaved as an adult." The woman flushed, compressing her perfect lips. "You look well, Louise." His voice gentled as he spoke, and his eyes did not seem to miss any detail of her appearance.

"Stefan. It has been a while, hasn't it? We can speak French if you wish," she said in that language.

"I would rather be understood by everyone. There has been too little understanding."

Bethany took a minute, as her ex-husband searched for words, to look over the man who had dominated her life and influenced so many of her decisions. Stefan was old. His tailor could hide the slight stoop he'd acquired in his posture and his barber could works small miracles with what little was left of his hair. Nothing could change the fact that he was growing old—and not gracefully.

"Louise—Bethany," he stumbled over her name. "I was told of this event and your involvement in it. I should not have been surprised to hear you and Phillip had come to know each other. Life has a way of doing strange things to one." He hesitated again, searching for words, or strength.

"I knew your father's lawyer. When you left, I went to him. He would not tell me where you had gone, only that you were well. I did not argue the divorce, with the understanding he would let me know if you ever needed anything."

"What I needed you could never give me," Bethany said, quietly but firmly.

He shriveled, and appeared even older. "I realize that. I never gave to you. I only took. What I did to you, and to your father, was unconscionable. It was the act of a man desperate to recapture his youth, indifferent to the harm it would cause anyone else. When your father was willing to give his own life away to save you from me I realized how debased I had become. I should have contacted you long ago, though I knew you would not want to hear from me. Leaving you in peace was the only way I could attempt to atone for what I had done."

Bethany thought of the years she'd spent worrying about this man. Now that he was in front of her, he didn't seem to be much of a threat at all. Secure in the love surrounding her, and in the strength she had attained within herself, she stepped forward, touching Stefan's arm with the tips of her fingers.

"You lived the life you had been raised to. I could very easily have fit into that life. You had no way of knowing it was not right for me."

Stefan took her hand in his, raising it briefly to his lips. "You could never have reached out to me before. You have become so strong, the woman you were always meant to be." He stared at her, sadly, letting the memories flow between them. Then he released her hand, turning to Jonathan. "There will be a wedding." It was not a question, but a demand.

"That's none of your business, Dubec," Jonathan answered smoothly, dangerously.

"Forgive me." The words came out hard between tight lips. "If there is a wedding, I would like to be there."

"We'll see." Jonathan slipped his arm around Bethany's waist, pulling her tight against him. She leaned into his side, waiting for her past to leave them for good.

Stefan turned away without further conversation, a sad old man who'd faced the reality of his life. With him went Jonathan's

TEACH ME TO FORGET

ex-wife, still staring daggers at the man who'd once caused her constant amusement. Their leaving was an event of minor notice to the small group.

"I have some business in town," Paul mentioned, scanning the crowd for likely prey. "Beth will need a ride back to her hotel."

Bethany pulled away from both of them, tired of manipulative males and confused by everything that had gone on. "I'll take a damned cab," she said, heading for the door.

"I don't think so." Jonathan's hand settled on her shoulder before she had moved two steps away from him. He drew her hand through his arm and held it firmly against his side. "Where's your motorhome?"

She glared an answer, realizing the futility of struggling.

"It's at my place." Paul answered, obviously amused. "Baron's staying at the clinic."

"Shame on you, Bethany. Leaving our child in a clinic." His voice teased, matching the unholy gleam in his eyes. She refused to respond. "Paul, I have to be here a while longer."

"No problem. I'll take care of the hotel. Marsha said she'd be glad to pack up whatever's there."

"Would you two stop it?" Bethany ground out.

Jonathan silenced her with a brief, hard kiss. "You're so cute when you sulk."

ℰↄℰↄ

"Are you going to pout all night?" Jonathan asked as if only mildly interested. He pulled the keys out of the motorhome's ignition and pocketed them.

Bethany refused to answer. She hadn't said anything to him since they'd left the gallery amid the curious stares of the people still there. Jonathan ignored her silence, remaining disgustingly cheerful during the long drive to Paul's, the reunion with Baron, the even longer drive in her motorhome. His own car, a newly painted classic Jaguar, was in the clinic parking lot, safely covered.

Now they were parked on a dark side road, backed up against berry bushes. Jonathan let Baron out, brought him back in and fed him. Still she sat in the passenger seat, hopeful, trembling, as he came toward her, removing his rain-beaded jacket. He looked at the bunk over her head.

"How do you pull this thing out?" he asked, still smiling.

That broke through her fog of insecurities. "I haven't used it since..." She was unable to finish.

ↄ⅁ↄↄ

The cheerful facade fled. "I understand," he said softly. He pulled out the bed, set up the covers and pillows before turning back to her. She remained absolutely still, her eyes large and still slightly shocked.

"Fantasy time, Bethany." He pulled her to her feet, removed her cape, then undressed her efficiently, ignoring the lure of her body. Hands at her waist, he lifted her onto the overhead bunk, urging her under the covers. "You'll get chilled, precious."

It was a matter of seconds to throw off his own clothes and slide into the bed, leaving the dim light on. Before she could become any more upset, he was next to her.

There was no time for finesse, no time for the practiced seduction he'd been planning for a month. There was only a frantic joining of two people who needed this affirmation of their love. Cautious of the low overhead, he pulled her leg over his hip, uniting them irrevocably in an explosion of passion.

Once their immediate need was satisfied, he rolled on top of her, effectively trapping her warm damp body with his own.

"There will be a marriage," he said, between kisses.

"Are you asking me this, or telling me?" Now she could tease, obviously secure in their love and future.

He flexed, rubbing his temporarily satisfied body against hers. "I could keep you captive until you agree."

"I could take a long time to make up my mind."

Jonathan raised himself on his elbows, cradling her head between his forearms, feathering soft kisses over her face. "What is it, precious? What's bothering you?"

"Jonathan, I'm not much of a housekeeper," she admitted, a frown gathering in her eyes. "You know how I cook. When I'm involved in a story, it can be even worse."

"Not to worry. We can both clean. I'll cook. If you want to eat, you'll have to be nice to me."

"How nice?" she asked coyly.

"Very nice," he said sternly.

She skimmed her long nails down his back, pressing them delicately into his flexed buttocks. As he groaned, sinking more heavily against her, she raised her face to meet his lips.

"Very, very nice."

EPILOGUE

It had been planned to be a storybook wedding. The bride's dress, in layers of pastel silk, complemented her heeled sandals. It had taken her at least fifteen minutes to arrange her hair in a becoming twist at the base of her neck. Unfortunately, the dress was badly torn when the bride ran into the forest, trying to rescue her sandal from the mouth of a red dog.

The bride eventually reappeared, dressed in ivory and emerald green. There was a slight delay when the groom insisted on taking the pins out of the bride's hair, letting it fall down around her shoulders. As they stood in front of the flowered podium, their attention was drawn to the back of the crowd, where a very wet red dog was happily drying himself on the expensive trousers of an elderly European gentleman, who was attempting to rescue what was left of a heeled sandal.

Finally, the vows were exchanged. As the minister solemnly asked if the bride would obey, she began laughing hysterically. The groom was forced to kiss her sternly.

THE END

About the Author

Mona Karel became convinced at an early age that her life would not really begin until she was about thirty five. She has no idea what precipitated that thought, but she claims she was a strange child. Until reaching that age, she led a peripatetic existence for many years, criss-crossing the country, working with horses and dogs—and waiting tables to support her other jobs. At thirty five, when many people are well into raising their families, Karel settled down to "real" work as a buyer and expediter. She married a high school teacher, which led to over twenty years in Southern California.

Karel can't remember a time she wasn't reading, though she doesn't remember much fun with Dick and Jane. Her preferred stories involved dogs and horses, and once she had gone through every horse book in the high school library, she started in on Civil War stories. They rode horses, didn't they? At that time Romance was swashbucklers and Gothic, and many preferred the stronger heroines of Mary Stewart and Victoria Holt. Then Karel discovered Romance in the form of Silhouette, Candlelight, and RWA, and her life was complete.